Journey in

By

Martin Heseltine

All characters in this novel are fictitious and any resemblance to persons, living or dead, is purely coincidental

The moral right of the author has been asserted.

ISBN: 9798685925077

Day One

Chapter 1

I

Adam Winter was reading through his notes. They needed to be clear and understandable, with no mistakes and nothing left out.

Notes

If, after reading this, you believe I've been stupid, I won't disagree. But I won't apologise for what I've done. I'm not proud of it, never that, but I wonder what you would have done in my place. I made a choice. This document tells the story of that choice, and of how I came to be public enemy number one. Not that there's a cat in hells chance of me being allowed my day in court; they'll do whatever's necessary to avoid such an eventuality, even to the point of murder. The reasons will become obvious once you start reading. So, this statement is my only hope of getting the truth out there and I really hope that you, whoever you are, will be my messenger. Maybe it's a long shot, I have no idea who you are, but I believe that any decent person would be sickened by what I've been through in the name of national security, and shocked at the involvement of those people we have trusted to run this country. I don't know how much time I have, very little I would guess, but this is written with pen and paper, because I don't trust any computerised system to be secure against government agencies. They have much more advanced technology than we do and finding me will be their top priority. So, I need to finish this before they find me. As they certainly will. No point kidding myself.

Some of what follows will doubtless be familiar to you; the media have recounted every riot, described each death, in exhaustive detail. Maybe you wondered why it all kicked off without any warning, or perhaps you just accepted the explanation from those in power. I wouldn't blame you for that. It sounded plausible, propaganda often does, especially as there were very few voices questioning the explanation of interference from a foreign power. At least, none that made the media.

But back to the beginning. You'll remember the virus. It was the virus that fired the starting pistol for everything that followed. Recognising this golden opportunity, those in power seized the moment and took full advantage of what our instructors called 'a gift from God'. Flames of fear were lit, fanned by a deliberate delaying of measures for controlling the spread, and the provoking of civil disturbances across the UK. Which was my role in events. This virus became the portal through which their genetic engineering project could slide unnoticed. Far-fetched? Really? Well, you must remember the terror of being in contact with other people, and the approving of draconian powers allowing the authorities to crack down in whatever way they felt necessary, all in the guise of keeping us safe.

Behind the increasing levels of infection and rising death rate were an elite group of powerful men and women, secretly working towards creating a smaller and more compliant population. Their ultimate aim was to micro-manage the hereditary process, by a weeding out of personality traits they found undesirable. Specifically, our instructors mentioned people with criminal records, those with no educational achievements, and others whose views were at variance with those of the state. Such was the long-term goal.

Power has little patience though and was unwilling to start a process which only their descendants would benefit from, so in the transitional period, the necessary genetic material would be created in a laboratory and injected into the population as soon as possible. Hence their delight at the appearance of a deadly virus.

There were six of us in the beginning, although I believe at least one was a plant to help ensure we moved in the direction they required. I have no idea if there were other groups developing alongside us, or if any went before or after ours. Their sales pitch was right on target, though. They knew exactly how to turn us on. Money and glory. We were to be twenty-first century guerillas, fighting a battle with weapons from the laboratory.

What twenty-five-year-old man could resist the challenge, the excitement, the guaranteed rewards? What else could my future hold that would compare? My parents were dead, and my long-term relationship had run aground several months earlier on the rocks of infidelity. Hers, not mine. Apparently, I was 'too serious and no fun'. Bad luck was hanging around me like a shroud. Two redundancies in the last three years, with little or no response from any of my recent job applications. Finally, I found work in a call centre, but they fired me for taking too many breaks. My last job was as a waiter on a zero-hours contract, which I lost after complaining about being sent home as soon as I arrived, because the restaurant was quieter than expected. My rent was in arrears, loan payments were overdue, threatening letters had replaced final demands. In our group we all had similar backgrounds and experiences. Feel sorry for me? Don't.

Their offer was irresistible. We were chosen to be a part of the vanguard, the scientifically created front line, individuals amongst the very few whose actions would be celebrated for eternity. None of us needed time to think, we all accepted immediately. None, as far as I know, ever questioned the morality of the state targeting biological warfare at its own citizens. Money creates its own rules. We were their lab rats, sent out to test the effectiveness of the genetic material they'd created. We were to be its front line, 'sowing discord, creating civil unrest, fostering hatred against any group that power deemed unnecessary for the country's future'. That was how they described it. Weaponizing individuals became the government's number one priority. We were Phase One, the trial stage.

You will, I believe, have seen the security briefings in the media. Cabinet ministers and civil servants repeating the mantras of 'hostile foreign interference in UK security', or 'it's the work of a lone fanatic'. It was neither of these things. I'm the evidence, my body the affirmation. I have traced this back to its origins, to the scientist in charge of the programme, who spoke to me about growing suspicions his work was not directed towards curing disease as he believed. During our discussions, Dr Robert Pritchard took me back further.

In the beginning was the idea. Whose idea it was, I can't even begin to guess. As I now understand, even behind closed doors, with rooms full of the government's natural supporters, the proposal initially faced massive opposition. As you would hope for in a democracy. Then deals were done, promises made, handshakes all round. Resistance evaporated as initial success began to win round the doubters, others disappeared. Long held desires for total and never-ending power suddenly seemed within grasp, a heady mix for would-be dictators. The possibility of their own lives never ending was the cherry on the cake. The convincer. Enough individuals bought into the scheme to make certain unlimited amounts of money were available with no budgetary constraints. No more Darwinism; this was no longer survival of the fittest, it became survival of those deemed by Power, to be the most useful. A new creationism was born. Eugenics. Selective breeding. Getting rid of 'defective stock' as they called it. Too many people making expensive and unsustainable demands on the public purse. Men and women who had never worked a day in their life having seven, eight, or nine children who would also grow up relying on the state. Criminals being cared for in prison. A breeding out of the poor and disadvantaged was needed. To be clear, this was nothing short of the murder of society. The chief scientist, Dr Pritchard, talked me through all the scientific evidence; most of it went well above my head, but it's on the memory stick included here. Get to him and he'll confirm everything in this document. He wanted someone directly involved, who had actively taken part in the training and in the field. That way, he said, we would cover all bases. They would have to believe us. Why he chose me, I don't know. I really wish he'd looked somewhere else.

But don't kid yourself. Don't imagine you're better or stronger than me, more virtuous, with stronger ethics and principles. Maybe you would have resisted? It wouldn't have done you any good. The point of no return is when they explain their plans. They chose cleverly. For someone in my position, Power holds all the aces. It can persuade and make promises, seduce and excite. Like me, you would be enticed by their approval - an experience rarely found in my life - and unable to resist their talk of glory and reward. Our names would be remembered forever, they told us more than once; the nation would be eternally grateful. And, as I said, once you knew the deal, there was no way out.

 So, I gave my pledge, agreed to their conditions, and signed on every dotted line they put in front of me. In return they gave me everything I asked for, every penny. A huge lump sum appeared in my bank account, so many noughts at the end, more money than I could have earned in a lifetime. No one had ever shown that much faith in me, so how could I possibly let them down?

There were jokes about guinea pigs. We all laughed along. But that is exactly what we became. Bodies to be experimented on, behaviour analysed, reactions to the drugs assessed. All marked down for future reference. On the ladder of research, I stood perhaps one rung above rats and mice. And who remembers their names?

Then came the virus, a perfect opportunity falling into their laps at exactly the right time, and these people knew how to seize the moment. How easy it became to convince the public of the need for universal vaccination, how expertly they teased everyone with reports of it being developed, then tested until, finally, confirming it was being manufactured. You will, I'm sure, remember this. Maybe, you were caught up in the general mood of fear. The clamour grew, the media pushed, demonstrators took to the streets. Power basked in the glory of producing the vaccine in record time.

How many people have any idea what any vaccination contains?

Becoming disillusioned as this entire pantomime played out in front of me, I began gradually withdrawing cash in preparation for the breakout I'd decided upon. My plans included Abi, although she knew nothing of it. Then events took over, I panicked, and believed that leaving her behind was my only option. It was a mistake. I regretted it almost immediately, but my bridges were burnt.

So, I know they're all looking for me. Their top priority will be my silence, at whatever cost. With their unlimited resources, all I can hope for is to delay the inevitable. Yet, there is one advantage I hold, one they can do nothing about. I have nothing to lose. So, there is this chance. This document and the memory stick. Whoever you are, please get this out in the open. Find Doctor Pritchard. Find Abi and tell her that I'm sorry, that my nerve gave out in the end.

Day One

Chapter Two

I

"I need you to find someone." The Controller's austere grey eyes stared directly at the younger man sitting opposite. "Quickly and with no fuss." Her mouth hardly moved as she spoke, as if she was forcing out every syllable. "This is a matter of national security." A high voltage flash briefly animated her poker-face. "And absolutely confidential."

"You said." Quinn stretched out his long legs and wondered why the room felt so much colder than the corridor outside. Glancing around the office, he felt a sense of individual and environment in perfect harmony. They belonged together, both were formal and uninviting. There were no personal photographs, no art works, and no luxuries of any kind. Her name was on the door, Claire Sharp, along with her title, but she could have just moved in that afternoon for all the personality it displayed. It reminded him of a police interview room - bare, vaguely threatening, and with no sound intruding from outside.

Her age was difficult for Quinn to guess. Fifty something he decided, her buttoned-up clothes and stillness suggesting watchfulness and secrecy. She wore no rings, no wristwatch; a small silver cross necklace was the only adornment to her dark suit. He tried to imagine her taking it easy on holiday or unwinding in front of the television. Maybe music did it for her, or detective fiction. But nothing peripheral seemed to fit.

"You will report directly to me." The Controller paused, her voice authoritative and firm, her face impassive. "And only to me." Leaning forward, her eyes never leaving his face, she pushed a card across the desk. "My secure number. You only ever use this."

"So why me?" Quinn pocketed the card without looking at it. His curiosity had been aroused by her voicemail, but his reply was delayed by his being away for a few days with his father, whose dementia was advancing rapidly. Care of the old man, now in his eighties, had fallen mainly on Quinn's younger brother Will and his partner Andy, a situation increasingly leading to arguments over family responsibilities. Now, Will had insisted they needed a break. So, although he despised his father, Quinn had felt backed into a corner and agreed to take him away for the week. He had chosen the Lake District as it was the only place he could recall the old man ever speaking fondly about. Why, he had no idea. As a family they had never been there; both his parents loved seaside resorts, and enjoyed the slot machines, cheap beer and dodgy clubs in the evenings.

Quinn had booked a hotel on full board in Ambleside, reckoning that at least the food would be sorted. However, the old man refused to eat anything other than eggs, or fish and chips, whatever time of day. At a loss for what they could do together, Quinn booked a boat trip on Lake Windermere, but his father had refused to climb aboard.

"Not safe," he shouted more than once, leading the tour guide to ask them to leave. No refund was available, further irritating Quinn. Twice, both during the night, his father had left the hotel and wandered off, the staff on duty denying they had any responsibility for keeping him on the premises.

"It's not a prison," was the response to Quinn's enquiry. "Just hide your room key." Both times, the police brought him back after a couple of hours. On his return from what he called 'the longest week in history', Quinn was fascinated by this contact, desperate to get back to work, and so accepted the Controller's invitation to meet.

"Don't you want the job?" He got the distinct impression from her sharp tone of voice that she didn't like being messed around.

"I just wondered." Quinn shrugged. "I thought you'd have your own people."

"We do." Leaning back in her chair, she sighed and briefly looked away. "And I don't like employing outsiders, but I need someone independent." Clearly, Quinn understood, this was a powerful woman used to getting her own way and comfortable with making decisions. If she were harbouring any doubts about him, he could see no discernible evidence. Nothing in her expression suggested any misgivings, or second thoughts. She wanted this to work, so Quinn pushed any doubts to one side. The question remained.

"Why me?"

"You've been recommended."

"Fair enough." Recommended? Who could possibly move in both her world and his? Contacts of a high-ranking government official and the desperate individuals drawn to his basic services seemed unlikely bedfellows. Still, he suppressed his curiosity, with every instinct and experience warning him not to ask for a name. She was highly unlikely to tell him and knowing the individual's identity would inevitably influence his responses both now, and during whatever job she had for him. But he would really like to know.

Forcing himself to meet her cat-calm eyes, Quinn began to find her stare unsettling. Never before had he experienced eyes blazing with such power; eyes he could feel probing every inch of his character, reading his whole life as if it were a book. Such eyes, he decided, were probably handed out from government supplies upon the reaching of a mandatory level of duplicity. He needed to be careful.

"The money's enough?" Finally, she cut through the silence, jolting him back into the room.

"It's fine." It was better than that. He'd been celebrating the figures since he first saw them, until it occurred to him that this wasn't charity, and he'd be expected to earn every penny. Once again, Quinn ran the numbers through his mind. It was eight times his normal charge and the Controller must know that. These weren't people who were sketchy on their research. He shrugged. "It'll cover a couple of bills."

"Or bring payments to your ex-wife up to date."

"You know about that, huh?" Quinn smiled. Of course, she had a file on him. What a compliment. To have the security services so interested in him, they needed to keep a record. He wondered, briefly, what would be in it, how big it was, how far back it went. How many times had she read it? An image of the Controller sitting in bed with a hot drink and his file in front of her brought a smile to his face, an expression he did nothing to conceal. Where was the evidence that he could be trusted to keep a secret? From whoever recommended him, presumably. Then why the file? Obviously, there were other candidates, so which specific biographical detail persuaded her to offer him this job? The brutality of his parents? His solitary nature? Or his short-lived police career?

Whatever swung it his way, it was just the controller who did the research and she alone that made the decision. Of that, he was absolutely certain.

"You thought we wouldn't check you out?" The Controller slid open a desk drawer and pushed a slim file towards him. "I need your signature on this document."

Quinn flipped open the cover and glanced at the first page.

"It places you under the requirements of The Official Secrets Act. There's a detailed statement of your responsibilities regarding this."

"Do I get to know the job before I sign?"

"No."

"A refusal would offend, I suppose." Ignoring her offer of a pen, Quinn used his own to scratch a signature, making it obvious that he wasn't bothering to read any of the document. The Controller scrutinized his signature and checked it against something on her computer screen but showed no reaction.

"So, what's the job? What poor bastard has upset you lot now? Crown Jewels been stolen? Some cabinet minister been caught with his pants down?"

"This is not a matter for levity, Quinn."

"I guess nothing in your world is." He leaned back, looked her straight in the eye, and tried to look comfortable.

"So I'd appreciate your serious attention." Her voice now sounded like ice cracking on a winter's day. "I have other important matters waiting."

"You had me at the money."

"Quinn." She leaned forward slightly. "Much of what I'm about to describe may seem to you as being part of some fantasy, or science fiction." She paused and just for a moment Quinn noticed the tiniest change flicker across her face, a slight discomfort, as she briefly chewed at her lower lip. Interesting. He filed it away for future reference. "However, I assure you that every word is true."

"Well, you've got me hooked. Does that mean I get every word, or will you be holding out on me?"

She gave no sign of having registered Quinn's comment.

"For a number of years now, this department has been developing strategies for maintaining the natural order of our society."

"The natural order from whose point of view?"

Again, the Controller paid no attention.

"Throughout history there have been many examples of how an external threat can be used to, shall we say, bring together a population in support of its government. I'm sure you don't need a list."

"No. I've lived through a few of them." He resisted the urge to challenge her use of the term 'external'. "Go on."

"So, to keep things simple, this department's brief was to find ways of promoting actions which would cause public opinion to turn against particular groups of people."

"You don't need to keep things simple." Quinn leaned forward, trying to keep his irritation from showing, wondering how much she was keeping back. "I'm a grown-up. These groups, who decides which are deserving of such attention?" If she caught the sarcastic tone, she gave no outward indication.

"We do, of course."

"Of course. Silly question." He paused. "Give me a for instance."

"I'm not sure that would be appropriate." For a split second, Quinn again thought he sensed discomfort on her face. If he had, it disappeared very quickly.

"Oh, come on. You checked me for recording equipment before I sat down. I've signed your bloody act. What am I going to do? Splash it all over Twitter? You'd put me in the Tower." His confident grin met her stare and he could almost see the calculations clicking through her mind. Surely, this 'need to know' had been decided before he got here.

"Coffee?"

"No thanks. It disagrees with me."

"Very well." She leaned forward and stared at Quinn. Something seemed to have got to her. "In general terms. Non-specific."

"That'll have to do I guess."

He watched as she gathered her thoughts. This must be a performance, he decided. Whatever she wanted to tell him wasn't going to be made up on the spur of the moment. That would be ridiculous. This was the centre of the UK's security services, deciding what to reveal on the hoof was hardly going to happen. Some deflection was going on here.

"Suppose we have a small but widespread community with a grievance against what they perceive as prejudice or injustice. They feel oppressed, subjugated, maybe even tyrannised and begin to make demands of the authorities. Changes in government policy perhaps, or the investment of public funds in support of their particular community."

"Would these be religious groups?"

"Possibly. But not necessarily." The Controller paused but didn't take her eyes off him. Quinn tried to keep his expression neutral and came close to succeeding. "Publicly, we make it perfectly clear that we have no intention of acceding to their demands. In private we offer them some hope. But only in extremely vague and general terms. 'When the time is right,' we say. Or 'We're putting measures in place'." She gave what Quinn assumed was a smile, one that didn't reach her eyes. "You get the idea."

"Then I guess you do nothing?"

"To begin with." Now he was looking for it, Quinn saw the slight discomfort flit across her face again. "Then we make it known all their pleas and petitions have been rejected. Out of hand. No further debate. We refuse even to meet with them."

"That would piss them off."

"That's not how I would put it, but essentially, yes." She paused, but Quinn made no further comment. "We make them as angry as possible. Then we go further and instigate, through a small group of specially trained agents, civil unrest within these communities, leading to protests, demonstrations and violence on the streets of our major cities."

"Clever."

"We then have a perfectly understandable backlash from the general public, demanding action."

"Stoked up by your friends in the media, no doubt." Quinn's voice became a murmur; press coverage of his dismissal from the force flared across his mind. Headlines he would never forget. 'Unfit to serve', 'Coward in blue', 'The filth'.

"Have you ever seen a magic show, Mr. Quinn?"

"Only on TV."

"As a child, I loved watching them and trying to work out how the trick worked." As she spoke, an image appeared in Quinn's mind, of a young girl dressed exactly like the woman in front of him, making notes in front of a TV screen, dissecting every trick, examining all its possibilities, then figuring out exactly how each deception worked. What then? Did she share the results of her scrutiny for the collective pleasure of her friends? Or revel in her superior understanding of a magician's deception? Quinn believed that, even as a child, the Controller would choose secrecy. "We know the magician is diverting our attention in order to complete the illusion of his purpose. Yet, it still works."

"We all fall for it."

"Indeed. And we are complicit in the trick. We want to believe it."

"So, the general public is distracted by the violence on the street. Allowing you to do what you want."

"I heard you were quick on the uptake. I'm delighted to see it's true."

"When rulers are in trouble, they start a war."

"Of course. In previous centuries this has been fought against a foreign enemy, these days it's easier and cheaper to set sections of your population against each other." This time, the Controller's expression wasn't what Quinn expected, but it was impossible to read. A quote came to his mind, he had no idea where from. 'No tyrant need fear, until men begin to feel confident about each other.' Or words to that effect. Something was missing, but he had no idea what.

"Bombs?" The thought suddenly exploded into Quinn's mind. That one word still had the power to derail him, to divert his mind to the memory he could never be rid of, the aftermath of the terrorist attack. The body parts, the screams, the panic. The end of his police career. Then the nightmares began, he re-lived those kids' bloody faces, heard again adults calling out their children's names. Saw once more the wretchedness of adults standing alone amongst the wreckage of a building that half-an-hour earlier had been filled with music, happiness, and applause. As the adults stared at one another, he knew what they were thinking. 'Please God, let it be their child dead and not mine.' The horror returned, as if he were still there, the fear that left him rooted to the spot, unable to do anything. Then his pounding blood as he ran.

Quinn had spent two long, lost years coming to terms with his feelings about that day. That one word was now the only trigger that could re-open his wound and bring back the shame he felt about his actions. He remembered the two years in therapy, the nightmares, the nausea and sweating, his emotional numbness and detachment from other people. His recovery had been hard, with slow progress to begin with, but Quinn knew he had to get through it. Everything his therapist had advised he had thrown himself into. He still walked in the countryside with his local group, still went swimming twice a week, still played his guitar. Confiding in someone other than his therapist Anne, was the most difficult part, even now talking about his feelings was a struggle.

"When you find yourself thinking about it, concentrate on something else." Anne's advice chimed in his mind. "Focus on what you can see or hear at that moment." It had worked, apart from that one word.

"Bombs?" Putting it into words, Quinn's voice trembled slightly.

"If necessary," she replied. Quinn felt the tremor through his body. These were not the words he wanted to hear. He'd hoped the Controller would say 'Never', or 'Not on my watch', or some other sympathetic phrase, but her actual words sent a chill through his body. She must know what had happened. That he had frozen when the blast was detonated, that he stood motionless, no more use than a statue, as people ran either towards or away from the explosion. That he stared into the distance, far beyond those standing in front of him, as they begged for help. All he could see was chaos, a pushing and shoving blur of movement, people fighting to either get away from the explosion, or run towards it. And that one woman, he would never forget for as long as he lived.

"She's only twelve," the woman screamed into his face, so close he could feel the spittle. "She was in there. Please help. Please do something." Sobbing, she grabbed him and pushed a photo into his face. "See. This is her. Katie. My daughter. Here, look. Please. Help me." The woman's face was distorted, tortured. He could see that, he knew, but he didn't want to know. He wanted to pretend he wasn't a police officer, just to get away from the bawling and the shrieking, from the shattering noise and the stench of fear. But the woman wouldn't leave him alone; she fell to her knees and clutched at his legs. Quinn kicked out and she released her grasp. Then, shamefully, he ran. Every instinct was telling him to get away, to run, to find somewhere away from those grabbing hands. He knew the memory would never disappear, but he had successfully distanced himself from that night and no longer beat himself up about it.

The Controller's expression gave nothing away, but Quinn knew she must be aware of that evening's events. His disciplinary hearing had been all over the media, but maybe the five years since then made it irrelevant. Not an issue. He hoped so. Maybe this assignment was proof it no longer mattered.

Neither spoke for what Quinn felt was an age but could only have been a few minutes.

"Okay." Quinn tried to discreetly wipe his sweating hands on his trouser legs, but he knew she'd noticed. Acting on the advice of his counsellor, Quinn diverted his attention to the money. "So, if you do all that shit, then why am I here?"

"One of our agents has gone off the radar."

"And you want him found?"

"That's correct."

"I get it." Quinn grinned, his mind now fully focused. "You want me to find him before your bosses find out he's gone AWOL. You wouldn't want a reputation for being careless now, would you? Pension at risk, is it? Damehood? Not too keen about working in Tesco, I suppose?"

The Controller said nothing. Impressive, he thought, her only reaction a slight narrowing of her eyes.

"On some job for you, was he?" Quinn felt the need to break the silence first.

"I can't comment on that."

"Yeah. Big surprise. I'm supposed to work miracles with one arm tied behind my back."

"Mr. Quinn." Her voice betrayed exasperation. "I have the funds. You need the money. Shows of bravado do not change those facts."

"I'll bear that in mind."

"Please do." She pushed an envelope across the desk. "Photographs, last known whereabouts, copies of passports and other documents." Quinn flicked through the documents. He glanced towards the Controller, puzzled, then looked back at six photographs on the desk.

"These are different people."

"They're not. They are the same person."

"But this one," he pushed the print towards the Controller, "is black. And this one," another photograph slid across the desk, "is a woman."

"Your observation skills are excellent, Mr. Quinn. Congratulations."

"Go on." Quinn leaned back again. "I can't wait to hear this."

The Controller pressed her lips together, creating a wafer-thin line as she made no attempt to disguise her annoyance at his flippancy.

"Have you heard of eugenics?"

"Was it a rock band in the eighties?

"I'll ignore your futile attempt at humour. It is, as I am sure you're aware, a process of altering the DNA in a living organism."

"Yeah. I know that."

"There have been many advances in this science. Crops can be created with a higher nutritional value. Animals can be modified for research purposes."

"Okay. So?"

"The science is complex but, in essence, DNA is extracted from one organism and combined with the DNA of another."

"Got it so far. I'll let you know if I'm struggling."

"Our scientists have recently developed the capability for using these techniques on humans, to facilitate changes in skin colour, body weight, age, and even gender. We add one thing, we remove another. A simple blood sample treated appropriately creates this flexibility."

Quinn's jaw dropped as he tried to concentrate. But it was so far-fetched, so much the landscape of science fiction, it had to be a joke. Right? It had to be some TV thing. A hidden camera, everyone laughing, waiting for the revelation.

"That's some impressive cut and paste job." After a long silence, Quinn finally spoke. It was all he could think of to say.

"A little over-simplified, but essentially that's how it works." As she replied, the Controller stared at a point behind Quinn. He could tell she was anxious to get this done but sensed that the practicalities were more problematic than she had expected.

"And the changes aren't permanent," she continued, now avoiding eye contact. "With this programme, one individual can become several entirely distinct and separate entities. It's an impeccable disguise. None of the wigs and beards so beloved by thriller writers. Each of our agents can have a number of completely authentic and realistic identities throughout their time with us."

"Shit." Quinn struggled to get his head around everything he was hearing. "Is this for real? You're taking a person, a real human person, and turning them into something else, someone else?"

"That's basically it. Yes."

"To do what you want. Like some human form of robot? Fuck. Double fuck." He spoke the last words softly, to himself. The Controller gave no sign of hearing.

"Initially there was an issue with producing merely physical changes." She was still speaking, quickly now. Was she anxious to get it over with, or excited by the material? Quinn couldn't tell the difference, couldn't concentrate, his mind was reeling all over the place. "But our latest developments allow the creation of altered memories, beliefs, interests. The body and the brain are altered and synchronised. This was the first big breakthrough, complete authenticity both inside and out."

"Whoa, whoa." Quinn held up a hand. "Slow down, will you?"

The Controller stopped and sat silently, while Quinn stared at the floor. He recognized the words. Every one of them. But they made no sense. New meanings were attaching themselves, creating monstrous images in his mind. And yet, the woman in front of him was obviously completely at ease, totally composed, speaking calmly. No wonder the money was so good. Could he do it? Could he really deal with this whole scenario? He could trace people and bring them back to whoever paid him. He had done that many times. It was part of his world, he understood it, even if sometimes he didn't agree with it. But this? An experimented upon individual who had gone AWOL for whatever reason, a creature with different appearances and, presumably, different personalities; where would he start? If he succeeded, could he really bring him back to face whatever consequences were waiting for him here?

"So, let me see if I've got this right." Quinn realised he would need to say something. "Your agent becomes part of a community, incites them to riot, so that you can scare the general public into responding with violence?"

"They generally don't need much persuading."

"To what end?"

"To avoid our society and beliefs becoming diluted with outside influences."

"War on the streets to keep power where it's always been." Quinn spoke almost to himself, wishing he could un-hear every part of her speech. When he looked back up, the Controller appeared to have a sympathetic expression on her face.

"I need to finish." She spoke softly for the first time. "The first phase has been completed. This was to create and then test the possibility of making people behave in certain ways. To investigate how certain attributes in individuals could be developed throughout the entire population."

"Attributes you wanted?"

"Of course." She smiled. "What else?"

"Yeah. What else?"

"So, we created agents with different characteristics, to enable accurate testing to take place. I need to stress that these agents were created by us; it didn't matter how we found them, we imbued every single one with the personalities we wanted."

"I understand what you've done." Quinn stood up. "I just don't want to be part of it."

"How about more money?"

"Don't you understand?" Quinn raised his voice. "No".

"Sit down, Mr Quinn," the Controller snapped and Quinn obeyed from sheer surprise. "Your personal views are irrelevant." She leaned forward and stared at him. "I would've thought you'd jump at the chance to redeem your reputation in official circles."

"Oh, I get it." He sat down. "Of course. That's why you chose me."

"Let me finish. Then I will try and answer any questions you may have." Quinn noticed the emphasis on 'try'. Without waiting for a reply, she continued. "My superiors are not patient. They demand results yesterday. By showing we could choose personality types, attitudes, and intellectual capability, in whatever numbers we chose, through simple injections, we created the ability to manage the hereditary process. Our values continue, those we disagree with don't."

"Go on."

"So, our sponsors are very satisfied. Definite proof has been provided. Individuals can be programmed to behave as the elite desire. Provoking riots did that, killing politicians did that, and so on."

"And creating these monsters took how long?"

"Initially, assimilation through this process took a number of months, too long for our purposes where we often need immediate action."

"Even God took seven days." Quinn stared at the cross around her neck, before endeavouring to focus his attention and concentrate on the words. Not the meanings, he told himself. Just the language. "So how long does it take now?"

"Once an identity is implanted, we can guarantee the entire process will complete itself within approximately thirty minutes."

"You're serious, right? You can completely change an identity, memories, body, beliefs, the whole shebang in the time it takes me to eat my lunch?"

"It still takes longer to implant an additional identity. Maybe, a week."

"That long eh? One week. Fuck. That must really piss you off."

"We're working on cutting down that time."

"Obviously." Frankenstein came to mind. But this was Frankenstein extra, Frankenstein plus.

No, plus, plus. "Your idea, was it? This creation of an army of freaks."

"No. I just manage it."

"And you still sleep OK?" Quinn stared in disbelief at the woman opposite, describing such dreadful activities as if she were discussing a new chicken recipe.

"Fine, thank you." Her eyes hardened. "Don't feign some sham holier-than-thou attitude about this, Quinn." She clicked her keyboard and glanced at the updated screen. "A man who's used blackmail, burglary, fraud and killing to earn a living? Somewhat hypocritical, I feel." She shut down the screen and fixed her remorseless gaze on him. "As I said, this is your chance for redemption."

An edgy silence settled around them, which the Controller seemed to have no intention of breaking.

"So, this explains the photos?" It didn't take long for Quinn to succumb. Raising his eyes to the ceiling, he cursed himself for such a weak question.

Of course, it explained the photographs. Stating the bleeding obvious, as his old boss used to say. "And why I'm here?" Even more pathetic, he realised. He needed to get a grip, if he was to have any chance of getting his head around this whole scenario. He was no saint, she had got that right. So, why didn't he just do the job he was being handsomely paid for, without getting involved in ethical questions that he could do nothing about? No government was going to change its policy on his say-so, and it would be a futile and very one-sided dispute. And maybe a shot at redemption was exactly what he needed.

"It does. To a point." The Controller's response surprised Quinn. "Are you sure you wouldn't like a coffee?"

"Scotch?" It was still morning, but Quinn sensed there were more revelations to come. What could top the current disclosure, he had no idea. But he knew a prop would help, and scotch was his normal support system.

"When I've finished. Your head needs to be completely clear."

"I've emptied it just for you." Quinn shuffled in his chair. "So, these photos?"

"It appears we were somewhat unwise to believe these genetic changes could be effected only under our control."

"Are you saying what I think you're saying?" A real punch to the guts. Just when he thought he'd heard the worst.

"To be clear," she continued, ignoring his question, "one particular agent has been able to regenerate independently." She leaned forward, clasping her hands. "This was a completely unexpected turn of events."

"I bet." Quinn's mood lightened at the thought of one individual throwing a massive spanner in the works. "Doesn't it fuck you off when underlings go off message? Start making up their own stories? Don't do the paperwork?"

"All I'm saying is that we have a problem with one of our agents. Nothing else."

"Just a shot in the dark. You want me to find him?"

"If you can stop wasting time trying to be funny."

"I'm guessing there's a complication." Quinn ignored her comment and spread out the photographs again. "To do with these."

"Well spotted. At least you're starting to think now." The Controller paused and looked directly for his reaction. "He could be any of those people."

Quinn looked over the photographs again.

"Is there any way of knowing which identity he's using?"

"An excellent question." She now had him where she wanted him and pressed her computer keyboard twice. "But no. There's no way we can be sure of that."

"So, he could be anybody, anywhere?"

"No. He can only use the identities we've given him. Those are shown in the photographs."

"Are the changes unlimited?

"We don't know."

"Great. So, it's like looking for a needle in a haystack when you have no idea what a needle looks like. Or even where the fucking haystack is."

"Rather dramatic, Quinn."

"Does he have money? A credit card? Cash?

"He's been withdrawing cash over the last few weeks." The Controller consulted her screen again. "It seems he's accumulated approximately ten thousand pounds."

"Well, that's a decent stake to carry around." Quinn whistled softly. "I reckon your best hope is that he gets mugged."

"He has four credit cards but hasn't used them for over a week." With apparent difficulty, she restrained herself from responding to his attempt at humour.

"And he won't. Different names, I suppose?"

"The details are here." She drew another sheet of paper from the drawer and handed it to him.

"I suppose we could wait until the readies are all gone." An oppressive silence settled over them. "Can I talk to any of the other agents?"

"Why? They're given separate missions."

"It may help discover something about his state of mind. Even prevent another agent from doing a runner." Quinn hoped his last comment would swing it. The Controller spent a few seconds considering his request.

"You can have thirty minutes in this room at four-thirty this afternoon."

"Without you?"

"Don't push it."

"Look, you've asked me to do this. I didn't ask for it and, frankly, I'd rather be looking for some missing wife or a case of stolen cash. But I'm going to do it, so you need to play your part. If I'm going to find this…this agent or whatever you call him, I'll need every bit of information about the consequences for those in this process. Their thoughts, desires. Fuck, I don't even know what I'll need, this isn't some routine missing persons enquiry. Until I talk to one of them, I won't know what'll help. You'll be a distraction. So, you stay out. One hour and I'll get what I can."

"Very well."

"I'll keep the photos." Quinn scooped them up and dropped them into his pocket.

"I want updates every twenty-four hours. More often when you get a lead. Any sort of lead. Understand?"

"Then what?"

"Then nothing. Your job is to find him. Don't approach him or make contact in any way. Find him. Report back. We'll do the rest."

After a momentary pause, she stood and held open the door.

Later that afternoon, Quinn sat in front of a screen. At the other end of the line was one of the missing agent's colleagues. No name. Just Number 9. He confirmed the Controller's briefing, almost word for word. He spoke about how getting used to a new identity took time, but afterwards the switching was easy. Number 9 didn't know the renegade agent and refused to speculate on his possible intentions. He also denied knowing it was possible to switch without returning to base. A frustrated Quinn finished the interview early, knowing he'd been unable to draw out anything of importance.

Day One

Chapter 3

I

"I need to know."

Switching off the TV where footage of the latest riots was showing, Abi turned to her friend. Abi's northern accent always seemed stronger when she was stressed or anxious. Sam recognized the signs, but Abi's forceful declaration still left her feeling off-kilter. This was the political Abi, the protesting Abi, but over a personal relationship. It was out of character and made no sense.

"You're sure he's gone?" Sam squirmed, watching Abi press her lips together and roll her eyes.

"Don't you think I'd know? That I haven't checked everything?" Abi's voice bristled, her green eyes narrowing like an angry cat. She gave a long, exasperated sigh. "His clothes are gone. Everything else too. Even photos off the wall." Crossing her arms, she leaned forward. "What would you think? Spring cleaning?"

"Sorry, stupid question." Sam looked away. "I wasn't expecting it, that's all."

"You weren't expecting it?" Abi clenched a fist. "How d'you think I feel?"

"No note? No explanation?" Sam's brow furrowed.

"Nothing." Distractedly, Abi ran both hands through her long red hair, normally so immaculate, but today dishevelled. Her clothes looked as if they had been slept in, which was ordinarily Sam's role in their relationship. Sam had always been slightly, and guiltily, jealous of the slender redhead's appearance, often comparing her own struggle with weight to Abi's ease within her own slim body.

"Not a thing." Abi stood and moved to the window as if hoping to see Adam strolling towards the Victorian terraced house that they'd shared for the last few months. She'd inherited the property when her parents were killed in a car crash a few years earlier. Adam had been Abi's first serious relationship since Sam had known her and their bond had grown stronger, the longer they were together. Her only other intense relationship, Abi had revealed one drunken evening when celebrating the sale of a painting, was with her college tutor six years before. After he dumped her, she discovered he was a serial womaniser, a fact apparently well known to the rest of her year, including those she thought of as friends. That none of them had bothered to tell her left Abi suspicious and unable to trust other people, pushing away anyone who tried to get close. At the time, Sam had been moved to tears, whether because of Abi's faith in her, or from too much drink, she chose not to dwell on.

"When did this happen?" Abi's hurt and anger were visible, understandable, and perfectly normal. But there was something else, something Sam couldn't put her finger on.

"Wednesday."

"Two days ago? Really?" Taken aback by Abi's news, upset at not being told before now, Sam bit her lip and held back before responding further. Too often in the past her knee-jerk reactions had made things worse, fueled misunderstandings with friends and created mutual suspicion. Sam was determined not to fall into that trap with Abi. Taking a deep breath and counting to ten as advised by her counsellor, Sam remembered Abi's earlier confidences, and smothered the stab of rejection. "Why didn't you call me? I could've helped. Looked for him, asked around, just something. Anything."

The two women had been friends since Sam had moved to the area two years ago, looking for a new start, and they first met while walking their dogs through the local woods.

They discovered a shared interest in music and by the time they parted Abi had agreed to give Sam piano lessons, in return for dog-sitting while she painted. As an arrangement it suited both women, but Sam found her progress was slow, gradually coming to terms with the fact that she was not a natural musician. Still she kept going, more for the bottle of wine they shared afterwards than from any musical ambition. The two dogs became firm friends.

"I'd been out painting by the river." Abi made no attempt at answering Sam's gentle rebuke. "I was really on it, you know. The colours, the shapes, just poured out of me on to the canvas." She turned back into the room, her eyes shining. "I've never felt it so natural before. So instinctive. It was incredible."

"And he was gone when you got back?" Softening her voice, Sam tilted her head slightly as she waited for her friend's response.

"I lost track of time. I had a lesson booked in, so I rushed back, and the girl was waiting by the door. We went straight into my piano room, she paid in cash, and we just picked up from where we finished last time. So, I didn't realise straight away that Adam wasn't there. It was only later, in the kitchen. His favourite mug was gone. The one with the Darwin stuff on it. You know."

"The four figures? From ape to human?"

"He loved the joke on the inside," Abi replied eventually, nodding slowly. "With the human going back the other way."

"I remember. It said, 'Go back, we got it wrong.'"

"Yeah."

"Well, I suppose…" Sam remembered Adam's often stated opinions on the collapse of social cohesion, his uncompromising views on how division between communities was tearing apart the world in which he grew up. He seemed to take it personally and became more outraged with each passing week.

"I just knew something had happened." Abi chewed at a fingernail. "He was always here in the evenings."

"Well, he took stuff with him, yeah?"

"Yes."

"So, he must've left voluntarily. Not been forced…"

"Look, Sam. There is something. He had a secret of some sort. I know that." Picking up her phone, she glanced at the screen before dropping it back on the table. "I just don't know what it was." She stood and began to pace. "I'm so fucking confused. I need a drink."

"Go for it." Abi's mention of a secret struck a chord with Sam, a bell ringing somewhere in the back of her mind. A vague recollection, like an old song drifting around the edge of her memory. No details, nothing concrete. She watched gin flow into Abi's glass from the already half-empty bottle of Gordons. "Just tonic for me." Sam grinned, tapping her midriff. "Still trying to lose a few pounds."

"I need to show you something." Some uncertainty had obviously been resolved in Abi's mind as her bewildered expression cleared. "Something weird. I found it after he…after Adam left." Abi drained her glass and poured another shot. Tonic fizzed from the bottle and gin spilled as Abi gesticulated frantically. "I don't understand it. What I found. I was just looking for some reason for him leaving, some explanation." She paced around the small room. "But this is inexplicable. It makes no sense." Abi stopped moving and squatted in front of her friend. "And I don't know what to do. Or what to think. And I don't like it."

"I can tell." Sam reached out and touched Abi's shoulder. She knew Abi to be naive, eager to believe and trust anyone who seemed to embrace her radical views. It had become Sam's mission to toughen her up, to help her identify the phoney from the genuine. There had been at least a couple of men in the short time Sam had known Abi, who had seemingly supported her beliefs, but just took what they could, then vanished into thin air. Maybe Adam was just another. Sam hoped not. "Please show me. Whatever it is. I want to do something." Speaking softly, she squeezed Abi's hand. "Maybe…a fresh pair of eyes… It may help."

Sam thought back over the few times she had met Adam, witnessing first-hand the almost embarrassing electricity between him and Abi. That instinctive reaching out to touch each other, the regular eye-contact, their obvious tranquillity as a couple, and she guiltily recalled the envy she felt at their closeness. The aura between them created in Sam a vivid sense of exclusion, an almost primitive awareness of their impatience to be alone.

Before Adam turned up, Sam had been Abi's only confidante. Being newly arrived and knowing no one, Sam looked forward to the time they spent together. It felt as if they'd known each other for years, so comfortable were they in each other's company. Conversations between them were easy, they laughed at the same things; Sam had never been so close to another woman. They were both only children with older parents. Abi had recently started to slowly open up about her feelings over the loss of both parents. A song playing in a restaurant caused Abi to stop eating and gaze into the middle distance, seemingly unable to move. Afterwards, she described how her father had loved the song, that they'd played it often, both dancing around their living room in gales of laughter. To Sam, it sounded idyllic, a million miles away from her own experiences of being locked in a cupboard for hours at a time, receiving a beating when her father was drunk, or his football team lost, running with her mother to a refuge when she finally plucked up the courage to leave. Sometime, Sam had decided, she would confide in her friend, but she worried about it tainting Abi's own childhood memories. Quite how it could do this, Sam hadn't yet worked out, but she refused to take the chance.

Watching Abi, Sam decided that a gin and tonic wasn't such a bad idea. It could even help. It had before. Would she suffer later? These days, she never thought that far ahead, too often her plans had been spoiled by other people. Besides, she had already called in sick in response to Abi's plea for help, so work wasn't an issue. The restaurant would undoubtedly survive her absence. Sam poured herself a large gin with a splash of tonic.

Relationships fell apart, Sam knew that better than most. Her lovers had usually been men already in relationships, on loan, often encouraged to stray by bored women. She found this to be the perfect arrangement, never pushing for anything more permanent, nor hanging around when such progression was occasionally suggested. Her own appetites were there to be satisfied, and she had no intention of sticking to the same diet forever. Jamie, her current lover, was no longer the funny, clever, and adventurous man she first invited into her life. He had become dull, self-obsessed, and controlling. The exit door was right in front of him, but he had neither the brains nor wit to recognise it. Michelle, his wife, was friendly, if a little stocky and in need of some advice about her hair. That she was reasonably attractive was important to Sam. Having sex with a married man, in some strange way she had never really understood, included having the wife in a weird kind of threesome. Sam could never bear to sleep with a man whose life partner was embarrassing, physically or intellectually; it would reflect badly upon her own attractiveness.

"OK." Draining her glass, Abi beckoned Sam to follow her upstairs.

"The stuff's in our bedroom." Abi led the way. There were two other upstairs rooms, the bathroom, and a spare bedroom where Sam had occasionally spent the night. Abi's piano room took up the annexe and had a separate entrance. The main bedroom was only slightly bigger than the spare and, Sam felt, intensely claustrophobic. Maybe it was the double bed dominating the space, leaving only just enough room for an adult to squeeze down either side. Or the large wardrobe with doors unable to fully open. Or the one small leaded window, closed at that moment, perhaps to keep out the rain lashing against it. Sam quickly noticed there was no handle for opening it. Shuddering as the room temperature seemed to drop, her breath visible, Sam began to feel uneasy. Moving to one side so Abi could close the door, she noticed there was a lock, but no key visible. If the door were secured from outside, there would be no way out. It's just an old cottage, she told herself. Built for agricultural workers, she remembered reading somewhere, among a row of four on the edge of town. Nothing out of the ordinary. Still, her apprehension stubbornly refused to disappear.

"Sorry, the heating isn't working." Abi shrugged apologetically, as she pulled open the wardrobe door as wide as possible, bringing Sam out of her reverie. Motionless for a moment, just staring into the wardrobe, Abi gave a brief glance at her friend, before reaching in and withdrawing a large brown envelope. Both women stared at it, then Abi took a deep breath and tipped the contents on to the bed. She spread everything out, before quickly checking nothing remained behind.

"Look." With her arms crossed, Abi gestured towards the bed with a flick of her head. "Go on. Pick one. Just look at it. Go on."

"What am I looking for?" Slowly rubbing the back of her neck, Sam's eyes darted between Abi and the pile of documents. Sitting on the bed, staring at the papers, her palms began to sweat as this moment collided with the memory of another time. Then, in a different bedroom, with other documents and photographs on a more familiar bed, Sam had discovered the truth about her parents. It was the last time she set foot in their house. Now, she tried to focus, looking at the papers, trying to decide where to start. Did that even matter? Should they be examined in some sort of sequence? No, Abi would have mentioned that.

"Just look. Please." Sam felt Abi's eyes boring into the back of her head, but before she could reach out for one of the documents, Abi leaned across her and grabbed a bunch of them. "Here. Go on. Look." She pulled at Sam's arm and forced the papers into her hand. "Look."

Taking the bundle, Sam stared at Abi uneasily. Her friend was twisting the sapphire ring around her finger and tapping her feet, a restlessness Sam had never seen her display before.

Normally, Sam loved uncovering information about people she knew. Not that she considered herself a gossip and would be horrified if anyone described her as such. In truth, Sam liked the power that came with such knowledge, but took little pleasure in passing it on. Once something became common knowledge, it lost all its clout. She knew Michelle was creaming off money from Jamie's restaurant, but had said nothing to either of them. Not yet. Sam liked to keep her powder dry.

"Go on. Will you just look. Read. Tell me I'm not mad." Abi raised her voice.

Sam looked at one of the documents Abi had pushed into her hand. It was a passport. Flicking it open, she became aware of Abi pacing around behind her. Who's this?" Sam held out the photograph. A black face, a name she didn't recognise.

"Look at the others."

A white woman, an Asian man. Different faces, unfamiliar names.

"I don't understand." Sam turned to face her friend. "Who are these people?"

"I don't know."

"Their dates of birth are identical." Sam looked at each document in turn.

"Really?" Abi frowned. "I didn't notice that."

Neither woman spoke for some time. The only sound was the constant hum from a dehumidifier underneath the window.

"If these are important, why didn't he take them with him?" Choosing her words with care, Sam looked through the remaining documents.

"I don't know."

"Where did you find them?"

"Just in the wardrobe."

"Not hidden?"

"No."

"Then either he left in a hurry, or he wanted you to find them." Replacing the papers in the envelope, Sam tried to sound upbeat. "We can't just leave them lying about." Making eye contact, Sam knew she needed to find a plan of action. Abi needed to be doing something, almost anything that felt that they were working towards finding answers. "I have a safe at home; we could keep them there until we figure out what to do with them."

"There's something else. In the spare room." Abi turned away and moved towards the door. Taking a deep breath, Sam followed her.

"Am I going to need another drink?" Only half-joking, Sam moved to stand alongside Abi in front of a small fridge on the floor. Kneeling, Abi reached right into the back.

"Secret store of beer?"

"No. Look."

Leaning forward, Sam stared at a row of four phials. Each was about half full of liquid. Each had a name on its label.

"What on earth…? What is this?" Sam furrowed her brow and stared. "Those names. They're the same as on the passports."

"Yes."

They stared at each other, Abi biting her lower lip.

"I thought I knew him, Sam." Shrugging, Abi turned away, tears welling in her eyes. "But now. With all this…"

"There's got to be a simple explanation." Sam closed the fridge door. "Or why would he leave them here?"

"I thought that. It shows he'll come back."

"We'll take these as well." Sam manoeuvred the fridge on to the bedroom floor. "I'll get my cool box. Temperature is obviously important."

Day Two

Chapter 4

I

The gun was pointing straight at Quinn. Behind it, a thin-faced man was grinning.

"Hey hotshot. Welcome home." He had a hard 'don't mess with me' voice and a red blotchy face that looked as if it had been stepped on. Several times. "Nice place." He glanced around. "You should lose the painting." He aimed at the wall-mounted Pollock print. "It's shit." It shattered as he shot. "I'd like a little chat with you."

"Well, I always enjoy an interesting conversation. Maybe we could discuss art as you have such strong opinions." Quinn's breathing quickened as he slowly closed his apartment door and pointed to the gun. "We need to talk about the tool first." He quickly assessed the space. The man wasn't close enough to risk jumping him, and his gun was steady. That 'stepped on' face was calm with no sign of nervousness. Tight-lipped, Quinn glanced around the room, faking a yawn. Photographs and papers lay strewn across the floor, empty drawers were discarded, his clothes scattered around. Having just left an angry exchange with Will, over the care responsibilities for their father, Quinn really wanted to take it out on this intruder but he forced himself to stay calm. "Maybe you need it because your conversation isn't exactly sparkling." He smiled. "I can see it would help stop people ignoring you."

"Comedian, huh." He jerked his head sideways. "Sit down. Over there."

Quinn did as he was told. The intruder remained standing but relaxed his arms and let the gun drop to his hip.

"This must be the bit where I ask what you want." Quinn stretched out his legs and gave a friendly smile. Since the bombing, Quinn took such personally threatening situations in his stride, almost enjoying showing himself the lack of fear he now felt. "And you say, 'I will ask the questions.'"

"Yeah. You catch on. And you answer them. Quick."

"Fire away then. Not literally, you understand."

"Funny guy." The thin man pulled up a chair and sat down opposite Quinn. Almost close enough.

"You've been given a job." The intruder prodded at the air with his gun. "To find someone."

"I get asked to find a lot of people." Quinn became transfixed by the veins throbbing in the intruder's neck.

"Not like this," he sneered, leaning back slightly and pushing out his chest. Off-balance, Quinn noticed, but still out of reach.

Looking him over Quinn found it difficult to judge the man's age. Mid-forties, by the look of him, ruddy complexion, dyed black hair. Dirty fingernails, he noticed as the man opposite lovingly cradled his gun. Hands with thick black hairs on their backs.

"You seem to be well-informed. Why don't you tell me?"

"Ever shot anyone, hotshot?"

"I've never felt the need."

"Well, there's no feeling like it. The buzz. It can be done quickly." He clicked his fingers in the air. "Or as slow as you like. Real gradual."

"You're the expert. I'll take your word for it."

"You're smart enough to know what I can do with this." He pointed the gun at Quinn. "So, spill the beans."

"I'm not sure which job you mean." Quinn smiled. "I'm a very busy man."

"Yeah, right. You're nothing special, hotshot. Just a big fat zero."

"You're going to hurt my feelings."

"Don't push it. You're looking for someone. My boss wants him first."

"And who's your boss?"

"You don't need to know that." The thin man smirked.

"Fair enough, but he must really be desperate to send an old loser like you." Watching carefully, Quinn weighed up his options. "What's it worth?"

"You get to keep breathing." The thin man's blotchy face turned a deeper red, and his eyes narrowed. "No deal. Nothing."

"Not much of a negotiator, are you?" Quinn really wanted to wipe that smirk from the other man's face but cautioned himself. Wait for the moment, it'll come. "Your mysterious employer must be willing to pay. Just to cover my expenses?"

"I ain't here to negotiate."

"Really? I never would've guessed."

The thin man stood and moved closer, pointing his gun.

"Listen, wise guy, you're going to start talking."

"Just like that?"

"Yeah." The intruder sneered. "Just like that." He stood over Quinn, his gun inches from Quinn's head. "Get this, Mister hot-shot P.I. Your choice. Toe the line or the first bullet goes in your foot. Then I work upwards. You don't die 'til I get to the head."

"Well, that's very persuasive. I need to get to my computer." Quinn pointed at the desk behind the thin man. "Thumbprint to open. It's all on there."

"Nice and easy." The intruder stepped to one side and nodded.

Quinn stood slowly and started to move forwards. The thin man was still in reach. Quinn spun quickly and punched him as hard as possible in the belly. The gun fell to the floor and Quinn kicked it away.

Then his knee smashed the doubled-up man's chin, before he slammed his right foot into the intruder's groin. Gratified by the agonizing sounds each blow drew from his opponent, Quinn collected the gun from where it had rolled and picked up his phone.

The Controller's team arrived quickly but with little fuss. They were obviously unsurprised and clearly experienced in their work, efficiently removing the unconscious intruder. Watching, Quinn briefly wondered what they were going to do with him but didn't ask. He wasn't that interested. Picking up the gun, he placed it in his desk drawer.

Once they'd left, Quinn poured himself a scotch and looked through the notes he'd made at the earlier meeting. There was no mention of any other groups that might be looking for the runaway agent. He sipped his drink, then leaned back and stared at the ceiling. The Controller could hardly have overlooked such a possibility, so it had been deliberate. What else had she left out? Who else could possibly know about the programme? Quinn poured himself another drink. This whole scenario was so mind-boggling, had thrown him so far off guard, he had failed to ask even the most routine questions. Taking another sip of his scotch, Quinn sat back down and again stared at the ceiling. The probability of his gun-toting intruder representing a foreign security service seemed high; the only other possibility he could think of was some campaigning group with a moral objection to the programme. Working on either premise, neither would give up just because a low-level operative had screwed up. Whichever it was, he felt sure their next approach would be much more professional. Most troubling of all for Quinn though, was the inescapable fact that someone close to the centre of this project was leaking information. It added up to a multiplication of risk Quinn could not get close to, and his fee suddenly seemed inadequate. For the moment, he decided to bury that banner headline. Distractions came in all shapes and sizes and Quinn recognised this was the complete works. The regular updates he had agreed to, were now as appealing as walking blindfold through a minefield but giving them a swerve would create a mushroom cloud of suspicion. First things first.

Switching on his computer, Quinn searched for images matching any of the photographs. There were five, three giving the name 'Adam'. Only one gave names for any of the other people around him. An attractive young woman called Abi Collier was pictured with him, four weeks earlier, at a climate change protest. Meeting Abi would be his next move.

II

Checking his watch, the welcome distraction of being due at The Brewer for his band's regular twice-weekly evening gig pushed the case to the back of Quinn's mind. It could wait. Quinn owed music and he knew it. He had a tab to pay. But it was a debt no amount of money could settle. For it was music that kept him off the streets after his dismissal from the force, music that got him through a painful divorce, music that helped him live again. Whether listening, or playing, or even just reading about it, music had been the power that healed and inspired him to carry on. Tonight's gig would free his mind from eugenics, switched identities, and security leaks. He felt it was going to be a good night. Or, at the very least, a relief.

Picking up his bass guitar, amp, pedals, and the ever-present photograph of his hero, John Paul Jones, Quinn had a last look around before leaving the apartment. All the other equipment, plus the set list, would be brought by his two bandmates.

The Brewer was 'a traditional venue', an inn serving local ales, a couple of draught lagers, cheap wine and various spirits. Crisps and peanuts were available for people requiring something to eat. Quiz nights, open mic evenings, darts and pool competitions, along with live music, all helped to keep the place open. As usual for such evenings it was packed; Quinn's band had a loyal following and could always be relied upon to fill the place.

The inn itself was the width of a standard retail unit, narrow but stretching back a long way. Above the public facilities were two further floors, each holding two residential apartments. The bar itself covered about half this length along the left-hand side as you entered. Floorboards and wooden tables were its only concessions to modernity. A sign on the door said: 'No children, no dogs,' which added to its appeal for regular customers. There were rumours locally that it was shortly to be closed in favour of a new, family-friendly bar/restaurant, something that Quinn felt was already well-catered for in town. If the place did close, then the town would lose a popular venue for live entertainment. But they were all aware that most people didn't venture out much for local performers, preferring to stay at home and watch well-known names on television. They were more comfortable with knowing exactly what to expect, he supposed.

'The Singing Detectives', as they called themselves, were setting up on a small stage at the back of the bar. The name was chosen because all three musicians worked in the sphere of crime investigation. Mia Wright on lead guitar/keyboard, was in forensics. George Baker, a police sergeant, played drums and the saxophone when required. Vocals were shared between them. Everyone, apart from Mia herself, recognized she had a genuine talent. When she was playing, the guitar seemed to form a natural part of her body; she was never flashy, no unnecessary fast runs, but holding back or letting rip when either was called for. And she had a voice made for the blues. Both Quinn and George were anxiously awaiting the day when she not only realised how good she already was, but also how far she could go. Neither man was under any illusion about who people turned out to see. Mia was already the star. If she gained confidence in her singing, she would be off and away.

The band's set list varied a little with each performance, depending on how much rehearsal time they'd managed to find, but they now opened with Bob Seger's 'Old Time Rock and Roll'. A few rockers, a couple of slower songs in the middle, then a rousing finish with a Stones number. Normally, they played nothing too recent; it was vital the crowd recognized every song.

At the end of their hour-long set, they had recently started asking for requests as an encore. Normally there were a couple they knew well enough but this time there were three, all requiring guitar solos from Mia. She didn't disappoint. Quinn stood transfixed along with most of the audience as her improvisation skills took centre stage.

George and Quinn silently exchanged worried glances as they packed away their gear in the van. Both knew what the other was thinking. All three then moved across to a table with their drinks. The buzz of performing had not quite worn off.

"Good crowd." Quinn grinned, leaning back, hands behind his head and legs stretched out alongside the table.

"More than usual." Straddling the chair, George looked towards Mia. "You seemed a bit preoccupied."

"Not really. I just felt we weren't really on it tonight."

"I thought it went great." Without moving, Quinn and George again exchanged glances.

"I've been thinking we should broaden out our set lists." Gazing vaguely around, Mia avoided eye contact with her band mates. "Push ourselves a bit. We've been doing the same stuff forever."

"People like it."

"Well, wait a minute, George." Anxiously, Quinn held up his hand. "Let Mia have her say."

"I'd like to write some songs for us to play."

"People need to recognize what we're playing." Staring at the table, George spoke as though stating the obvious.

"Well, let's think about this." Quinn leaned forward, keeping his eyes on Mia in the hope of seeing her response before she said anything else. "We could start off with one or two, in the middle, and see how that worked."

"We can talk about this later." Standing, Mia collected her bag and moved to join a young woman at the bar.

Day Three

Chapter 5

I

The two men were watching the six-o-clock news. They didn't have long to wait as the expected report was the programme's lead item, even taking precedence over coverage of the latest riots. The room itself was above a pizza restaurant, its basic white wallpaper peeling in places and stained in others. Packing cases formed two chairs and an old card table sat between the pair, upon which sat the small portable TV set and an uneaten slice of pizza.

"A body, thought to be that of missing scientist Dr Robert Pritchard, was today discovered in a wood close to his home." The presenter spoke concisely, direct to camera, his face solemn. "We can now go over to our reporter at the scene."

"Yes." The unsmiling female reporter held a microphone in her left hand and occasionally glanced down at some notes held in the other. "Dr Pritchard has been missing for two days. The body was found early this morning by a dog walker in a secluded and isolated area of woodland close to his home. She was attempting to retrieve her dog after it had run off." The reporter consulted her notes. "The cause of death is not yet known as the forensic team is working on the body at this moment." She moved slightly to one side and indicated with her right arm. "You can see their screens behind me. The police have requested that we do not speculate at this time, but they'll be issuing a statement later this evening."

"We'll hopefully have more on that story in our bulletin at nine-o-clock." The newsreader smoothly moved on to the next item, covering a demonstration in central London that had spiralled out of control. Unrest was growing over the government's decision to deny residency to worshippers of any religion, other than Christianity.

"You left no trace?" Hacking switched off the television, his voice expressionless. An aura surrounded him, a sense of strength and power, which drew people into his orbit. To the casual observer, he could be mistaken for an accountant or solicitor, for he was tall and always immaculately dressed. Those who had business dealings with him, however, would never make that mistake. Neither would anyone getting close enough to look into his eyes. Ever-vigilant eyes, dark and hard as daggers, eyes that were now fixed on the thin man. "I don't need to get you out of a jam again, then?" He leaned towards the other man. "Not like the mess you made with the private detective?"

"Nah. Left nothing." With a sulky expression, Rader stared at the table. "And anyway, I got the tracker on Quinn's shit car, didn't I? So not so fucking useless."

"After I intervened and sorted your release."

"Still did it though."

"Well, anyway. This job has definitely been completed successfully?"

"Yeah. Like I said." Rader looked up, grinning. "Smashed it. Sweet a nut." Hacking's irritation was not assuaged by the predictability of Rader's boasting.

Hacking loathed men like Rader, faithless people who would do anything for money, whose only ambition was to find a fix to satisfy their immediate desire, just so they could then move on to the next depravity. He hated the aroma they all seemed to share, a putrid contaminated smell, suggestive of their souls decaying, and which seemed to strengthen after every job. It even applied to the women and Hacking had noticed an increasing number willing to participate in acts of profanity for cash. Not that he had employed any yet.

Unpleasant though it was, Hacking had no choice than to deal with such people; they were essential to the services he provided, and a necessary evil for dealing with those whose power encouraged actions contrary to the word of God. A love of money was the sinful root cause, he understood, which is why his own lavish lifestyle was so important. It provided conclusive proof that those with true faith could reap rewards far beyond the reach of the selfish and ungodly. Often, Hacking used the biblical quote from Matthew 19:24 that 'it is easier for a camel to pass through the eye of a needle than for a rich person to enter the Kingdom of God'. He would question their understanding of this statement, then point out how it was often used to mislead people. The true meaning of these words only became clear through further Bible study, the meticulous Hacking would explain. Hoarding riches for oneself is the problem, he clarified, which does present a barrier against entering The Kingdom of Heaven. And a very considerable barrier. By comparison, he went on to enlighten his audience, those wealthy individuals who channelled money regularly through a recognised spiritual organisation, were guaranteed a fast-track into Heaven. Luckily, his own devotional group, The

Divine Path, provided such peace of mind. To facilitate this guarantee, new members paid a lump sum upfront, in addition to regular monthly payments, which were individually calculated as a percentage of the devotee's income. This was assessed and renewed annually.

This level of contribution from disciples of The Divine Path ensured the group's dedication to providing followers with advice and assistance in finding the one true route into heaven was fully funded and immensely profitable. By continuing his other business, Hacking would explain, it set an example about the importance of work and the sin of idleness. This had become a frequent subject of his irregular sermons at The Divine Path's monthly gatherings. Hacking was passionate in his belief that Christianity should not be a spectator sport, just turning up and watching what happens, listening to the readings, having a cup of tea, then going home. It should not be passive or comfortable. It needed to become more active in promoting the message. He had studied the Crusades, where Christians reclaimed the Holy Land from Islam. The Knights Templar provided his template for The Divine Path; they were fearless and fierce fighters, slaughtering those with different beliefs, building up huge wealth and indulged with special privileges. Hacking compared this to the docile and submissive Church of England and knew he had been called upon to act. Ends justify means, he believed, and at his fingertips were killers, blackmailers, and thieves, all happy to ply their trade for money. To begin with Hacking had tried to convert them, but soon realised that would only deplete the resources available for his work.

Having discovered, from one highly placed devotee's inadvertent revelation, exactly what Dr Pritchard had been working on, Hacking had felt sick and appalled. It was pure evil, an abomination far beyond any he had previously dealt with. To claim the power of creation for mankind was the work of Satan and had to be destroyed.

"Well, then." Hacking leaned forward. "Tell me how it went."

II

Rader was ready for this. Hacking always wanted chapter and verse, like he got off on it, and this irritated him. None of the other people he did jobs for had any interest in minute details. If the job was done, that was all that mattered. Hacking could get off his arse if he wanted to find out stuff, instead of sitting in front of a computer. He paid well enough, but so did others. And they didn't preach at him. Nor, if he arrived late, did he find them reading the Bible. Maybe 'The Racing Post', for tips or 'True Crime' for ideas, but nothing else. So, on his way to the meeting, Rader rehearsed the report he would give. He believed every angle was covered; he had considered every possible eventuality and arrived at a convincing plan. He would give no details that may be contradicted if more specifics come to light; keeping it vague was essential. Revealing the truth was out of the question. It could complicate the agreed payment and may even jeopardise future contracts, as Hacking was just the sort to quibble over minor details. The target was dead, why did it matter who had done it? Rader was on site, hiding in some thick bushes, silently cursing their scratching barbs along with the incessant drizzle, waiting impatiently for his chance. He had been in position, ready to strike, on the point of dispatching the doctor into whatever the hereafter held for him, when a stranger meandered into view. The sight of this trespasser did nothing to improve Rader's mood; he had wanted the job done in time to get back for a vital darts match.

The stranger's face was obscured, partly because it was almost dark, but also because he was wearing a scarf and low-brimmed hat. The two men seemed to know each other, as an exasperated Rader watched them have a brief conversation. Then the doctor fell to the ground, and the stranger leant over him, before turning to stroll away. Nothing about him suggested he was in any hurry. For an eternity of seconds, Rader remained in the bushes, his jaw clenched, uncertainty clawing at his mind. Eventually, he carefully pushed some greenery to one side, pulled out a thorn from his sleeve, and cautiously peered out. Nothing was moving. Waiting to be sure the stranger wasn't returning, Rader moved slowly towards the prone figure. A quick glance confirmed the target was dead. The other man was nowhere to be seen and Rader was alone with the body.

Making up his mind instantly, he photographed the body, then quickly moved away. Only he had seen the other man, of that he was certain, and it was unlikely the stranger would come forward voluntarily, so his own version of events would be all there was. If they believed he had carried out this mission with such efficiency, his reputation would soar. Praise and admiration would be heaped upon him and his services would attract a premium on top of the normal fee. It was a win-win situation. A no-brainer. The only unsatisfactory part was that he missed the violence, the adrenaline surge of physical power over another person. That was his drug. Ever since that night he would never forget, watching the older brother he adored being beaten, tortured, and killed by four men. Too scared to leave his hiding place, the thirteen-year-old Rader had forced himself not to cry for fear of attracting attention. He had never cried since, not even when his mother died. But he forced himself to watch. He knew the men. Every one of them. He watched what each of them did, memorised it, replayed it in his mind almost every night. The police arrived, asking questions that no one answered. They poked around the back alley, collecting pointless bits of evidence which they took away. Watching them, Rader could tell they weren't really interested; to them it was obviously just another ghetto killing. One more drug dealer off the street. Rader waited three years, watched as the killers built an empire selling drugs, expanding it into neighbouring towns, always moving around, dripping with jewellery, and driving fast cars. At sixteen, he killed each of them in turn, very slowly, over one hot summer. Every minute of their suffering electrified him, and ecstasy washed over him as each gasped their final breath. Nothing had ever come close to that thrill. There was no connection between Rader and the four men, so no reason for the police to talk to him. But every reason for him to seek out opportunities to get that buzz again. Which is why he felt cheated by the killer of Dr Pritchard.

"Then that solves one problem." Hacking looked at the photo and gave a tight-lipped smile. "Maybe you're not so incompetent after all."

"Sweet."

"Your next job," said Hacking. Rader glanced at the typed sheet of paper before pocketing it and leaving.

Checking his phone as Rader left, Hacking realised his next steps would need to be carefully thought through. One scientist was dead, which would cause a delay but no more than that. Hacking had already identified Doctor Moss, a member of The Divine Path, as the perfect replacement, whose job would be to ensure Christianity was part of the engineering process. All that was needed now was a way to persuade Moss, in the unlikely event of him putting up any objection.

III

A few miles away at her Chelsea home, the Controller was also watching the account of Dr Pritchard's body being found. When the report finished, she muted the sound and picked up her phone.

Within a few minutes, she was joined by two senior members of the security services. This wasn't unusual, the Controller often held sensitive meetings at home, because it attracted less attention. They were never disturbed, she was unmarried with one estranged brother, Carl, who lived in the South of France. They no longer exchanged birthday or Christmas cards and hadn't spoken for many years. The Controller remembered an angry and one-sided telephone conversation, where Carl itemised his many reasons for loathing her and the work she did. Coming to terms with never having any contact with her two nieces had been painful to begin with, but no longer troubled her.

What surprised the Controller wasn't the arrival of Sir Anthony Cardew, after all he was the chief advisor to the government on security matters, but the young woman accompanying him.

"Evening, Claire. This is my assistant, Kristina. With an unpronounceable surname." Not looking at either woman, nor waiting for any response, Sir Anthony made himself comfortable in the living room. Shrugging and giving an apologetic smile, Kristina followed.

"I've met Kristina before." Smiling she turned to the other woman. "How are you?"

"We need to concentrate. The work must continue," Sir Anthony interrupted, giving Kristina no opportunity to reply and speaking before either woman had sat down. There was no preamble, no social niceties; this was not a man interested in small talk. As usual, Sir Anthony sat with his legs wide apart and leaned forward when speaking, hands clasped together in front of his knees, always determined to be the centre of attention. A divisive figure, married to the job, he liked nothing more than a crisis, especially a crisis he could claim to have seen coming and one in which he could also apportion blame. In his early fifties and unmarried, unsurprisingly in Claire's opinion, Sir Anthony was not a career civil servant, but a political appointment. It came completely out of the blue; there had been no discussion about the need for such a role, no process for the selection, and he had been ruffling feathers for more than three years.

"I'm here to cut through all the bullshit." Claire vividly remembered his words when they first met. "Put a rocket under your cosy little department." Afterwards, she returned to her office and hunted for information about him. There was surprisingly little. He was privately educated, followed by St. Andrew's university where he was awarded a 2:1 in 'Public Policy'. From the little information available, he seemed to have been well regarded by his tutors, gaining a reputation for independent thinking and for getting things done. Less positively, from Claire's point of view, he was also described as being overbearing and dismissive of those who disagreed with him. After university, he became a publicity-shy entrepreneur with several business start-ups to his credit, mostly in hi-tech industries, Artificial Intelligence being a particularly noticeable interest. There were some reports of employee dissatisfaction at their terms of employment being changed without consultation, but he had become a multi-millionaire. By the time of his appointment, his business relationships were spread throughout the world, with easy access to those in power. His role as an advisor to the government was wide-ranging from the start, spreading across all departments. Like a virus, Claire thought, but she kept that to herself.

Claire remembered meeting Kristina's parents. They hadn't stopped smiling once, their pride in their only child was obvious, delightful, and fully deserved. Kristina had progressed extremely well, working tirelessly, and gaining regular promotions. They'd hardly paused for breath while telling Claire about their daughter's other achievements. A first-class degree, playing the organ at the church they attended, and volunteering at a dog rescue centre. Claire guiltily remembered cynically wondering if Kristina had any bad points, before blaming the job for making her so distrustful. Observing the young woman sitting in front of her now, Claire sensed that the dark blue suit was something she felt imprisoned in, rather than had chosen to wear. Vibrant colours and casual clothes surely would be more to the young woman's taste; her bright red lipstick and undisciplined shoulder length fair hair suggested a small but defiant air of rebellion. Sir Anthony would do his best to get rid of that, she decided, but could he control any independence that lay behind it?

Avoiding Sir Anthony's weapons-grade glare, an expression under which most subordinates visibly wilted, Claire knew exactly what he would say next.

"This is a national security issue."

"Of course." Having experienced this patriotic card being played more times than she cared to remember, Claire again felt that in the interests of truth, the words 'career path' should be substituted for 'national security'.

"You presumably have a successor in mind?" Leaning further forwards until he seemed to be challenging gravity, Sir Anthony looked towards Kristina, as if checking she was paying attention. "We have no time for some long drawn out recruitment process."

"Of course."

"Remember," he continued, in a tone more threatening than Claire felt was necessary, "you have a responsibility to ensure the correct appointment is made."

"I take my responsibilities very seriously." Her shoulders tensed. "You can be assured of that."

Watching as Kristina leaned across and whispered in Sir Anthony's ear, before smiling as she sat back, Claire shuddered involuntarily. That close was far too close.

"And the appointment needs to be made quickly."

"I am aware of the urgency, Anthony." Deliberately Claire omitted his title, knowing he insisted on it being used in all meetings, smiling as she noticed his body stiffen. "Logically, it should be Dr Moss. He's been working alongside Dr Pritchard throughout this research."

"I need to be reassured he doesn't hold the same perverse views as Pritchard. We can't afford another loose cannon." He banged his hand down on the small table, the sound ringing around the room. Knowing there was more to come, Claire waited as Sir Anthony took a deep breath. "You were responsible for the appointment of Pritchard, were you not?"

"As you're well aware."

"Yes. As are those on the top floor." Either he was grinning or had a stomach upset, Claire wasn't sure which.

"Is that a threat?"

"You can decide that for yourself." He leaned back, smiling. Kristina looked down and away to the side.

"Dr Moss is extremely highly thought of and committed to his career and family." Wondering what the young woman was thinking, Claire's eyes narrowed but she kept her voice calm. "He will present no issues with independent thinking and will be available for full vetting."

"I now have the authority to veto this appointment, should I not be satisfied." Smugness arrived, a little earlier than Claire expected. For the first time, Kristina's eyes met hers.

"Then maybe you should make the selection."

"That wouldn't be appropriate."

"I see. Authority without responsibility."

"Shall we move on." Kristina lifted her jaw.

"That may be best." Claire was intrigued to hear what the young woman had to say but looked directly at Sir Anthony. "If that meets with your approval?"

"Go on." Gesturing towards Kristina, he leaned back. "Go through the science. We can come back to the appointment issue."

"I am aware of the science."

"Carry on, Kristina." Sir Anthony reached into his pocket, took out his phone, moved away from the two women, and started to scroll through his messages. He answered one call, his words inaudible to Claire, before leaving the room.

"That's fine," Claire muttered. "Just wander around my house as you see fit." If Kristina heard, she gave no sign.

"I think we should wait for Sir Anthony, don't you?" She flashed a dazzling smile. "We don't want any misunderstandings."

"As you wish."

Leaning back in her seat, Claire studied the self-assured Kristina. Her obvious comfort and remarkable lack of haste were impressive, suggesting Kristina wanted Sir Anthony to hear what she was saying. Most officials would do anything to avoid him listening to any briefing they were giving. They even looked uncomfortable running Q&A sessions.

"But while we're waiting," leaning forward, Kristina smiled, "can I just emphasise the importance of regularly re-visiting our goals. It helps prevent us losing focus on our end-game."

"Absolutely."

They sat in silence for some minutes, until Sir Anthony returned with an angry expression. He made no apology for the interruption.

"We decided to wait for you." Kristina looked over her shoulder towards Sir Anthony. "I was just explaining the importance of re-visiting our goals."

"You needn't preach to me." Shuffling in her seat, Claire realised she sounded more impatient than intended.

"Claire," Sir Anthony resumed the same pose as he sat back down, but his demeanour had changed, "will you do me the courtesy of listening to my colleague. This is not a game. Our national security interests demand you take this seriously."

"I understand that." Claire indicated Kristina should continue. She recalled a quote from somewhere, 'Patriotism is the last refuge of a scoundrel' and became distracted with trying to identify its source.

She had to force herself to listen, once more, to the PR version of what was happening. A positive spin for politicians, an easy media success guaranteed to raise profiles and increase popularity. The project was based around scientists developing a new gene therapy technique, enabling the transformation of human cells into mass producers of tiny Nano-sized particles full of genetic material with the potential to reverse disease processes. It would pave the way for curing cancer, Parkinson's disease, anxiety, and a whole lot more. Kristina was convincing, almost evangelical, so much so that Claire wondered if she really believed the words she was speaking.

"This is just for show," Claire interrupted, slightly distracted by Sir Anthony pacing around while checking his phone messages. "Or am I mistaken?"

"Well. Of course, research of this nature does bring many benefits."

"It's how we maintain our funding." Looking up from his phone, Sir Anthony's glare moved up a notch. "And it can be used for those things."

"Can be?" Claire wondered if anything she could say would wipe that self-important and self-satisfied expression off his face. She doubted it.

"Obviously, the treatment will be expensive." Kristina tilted her head and smiled again.

"Obviously."

"Research costs are incredibly high."

"It's a question of funding, as I'm sure you are perfectly well aware." Sir Anthony was not a man to leave a gap in any conversation. Delighted she had at least made him put his phone away, Claire remained silent. "Research into controlling diseases goes down very well with the voting demographic," he continued, puffing himself up. "Politicians don't want to know what we do. They just want to look good, to get re-elected, to get in the shop window for some high reward consultancies or directorships. So, whatever it takes to keep our funding is what we do." He seemed to feel that settled the matter, leaning back in his chair, as if trying to give the impression of total relaxation. But his eyes didn't stop moving, even after indicating to Kristina that she should continue.

"And the other side of this research, Anthony." Claire spoke before Kristina had the chance, her expression neutral, apart from a slight smile at the edge of her mouth. "Shall we call it the dark side? I rather like that phrase and I believe you've used it on more than one occasion."

His apparent unease was so brief, it could easily have been missed, but Claire was watching closely. His anger though, was perfectly obvious. Kristina seemed puzzled.

"Our research programme will play a vital part in creating a population with total allegiance to the state. Social stability comes from individuals all working together, with the same beliefs. We know liberal democracy is dead, no recent UK government has been able to govern properly. Too many regulations, vested interests, too much red tape. This project is now the government's top priority. Proper planning for the future needs of the state. Offering free health care and education for all is a ridiculous waste of resources." His speech became quicker. "What an opportunity we have. No unemployment, no free loaders. No homelessness. There are far too many people draining the public purse. You know the reasons. It's completely unsustainable for the hard-working people of this country to pay taxes to support parasites, dead-beats and the work-shy."

"And we set the goals?"

"Of course we do. Who else could do it?"

"So, no freedom of choice?"

"It's an illusion, a fantasy. Always has been."

"I see."

"Claire, are you onboard with this project, or do I need to replace you?"

"I've very successfully managed this programme since its inception, Sir Anthony." Her face remained impassive, although a slight flush appeared on her cheeks. "Do you believe I should be blindly following your orders, or is it still possible for me to ask questions?"

"I don't think," Kristina looked towards Sir Anthony before speaking, "that anyone believes in blindly following orders. Questioning helps to ensure we've covered every base." Watching Kristina closely, Claire could clearly see how rapidly she'd developed. Her self-assurance was impressive. "And this is a crucial moment, as we're almost ready to move into phase two."

"I see." Claire looked from Sir Anthony to Kristina and back again, and saw conviction burning in his eyes, but something much more subtle in hers. "So, the first phase has been successful?"

"Absolutely." As Kristina smiled, her blue eyes gleamed irresistibly, almost distracting Claire from her words. "Your agents have proved beyond any doubt that genetic engineering can be micro-managed and successfully targeted directly at control of a small group and then influence an entire community."

"I'll take that as a compliment."

"Don't get too carried away, Claire," Sir Anthony snapped. "You've not been entirely straight with us."

"Sorry?"

"You've lost track of one of your agents."

"One has recently gone off-grid, yes."

"You didn't think it worth reporting?"

"If I reported every little thing…"

"Little thing?" Sir Anthony roared. "You call that a little thing?" Standing, he once more began to pace around, his face red, veins throbbing in his neck. "I'd say it's a massive fucking thing. It puts the success of this project at risk." He stared directly at Claire. "Are you really so fucking stupid?"

"Agents sometimes go silent." Struggling to keep her voice measured, detecting an obvious increase in his stress level after dealing with his phone messages, Claire was surprised both by his knowledge and his swearing. Glancing towards Kristina, who was looking at the floor while gently pulling at strands of her hair, Claire took a deep breath. "It happens. They become attached to someone, get sick; there are any number of reasons why they're out of contact for a short time."

"You've engaged the services of a private investigator, though." Kristina frowned. "Rather than use our own people."

"You really wanted to keep this a fucking secret, didn't you?" Sir Anthony finally sat down. "You're paying him a fortune."

"Budget cuts. We had no one suitable available."

"I can easily check that."

"Please do."

"Perhaps a coffee would help us all calm down." Smiling cautiously, Kristina glanced at the others.

"I don't need to fucking calm down, but I'll have a coffee."

After a few minutes, Claire returned with the coffee. Sir Anthony and Kristina broke off their conversation as she entered the room.

"Biscuits?" Sir Anthony spoke while looking at his phone.

"I don't have any, I'm afraid." Resuming her seat, having overcome her irritation at Sir Anthony's awareness of Adam's disappearance, Claire looked at him with expressionless eyes. If Quinn did his job, none of this would matter.

"No problem." Kristina said. "I need to cut down on the sugary foods."

"We need to discuss Pritchard." Sir Anthony poured himself a coffee.

"Before we do," Claire waited for Kristina to follow suit, unsurprised neither offered to pour hers, "can I just confirm you wish me to fully brief Dr Moss?"

"Within the limits of his security clearance." Kristina sipped her coffee.

"Pritchard began to express doubts." Obviously keen to move on, Sir Anthony was now much calmer. "Instead of just doing his job, for which he was very well rewarded, he talked openly about anomalies, and areas of research that made no sense to him."

"I seem to have been kept out of that particular loop." Claire waited, but there was no response.

"We believe he was ready to go public with his thoughts." Speaking slowly and choosing her words with obvious care, Kristina kept glancing towards her notes. "We found copies of documents at his home, some clearly setting out what you call the dark side of this research. Much of this information he had no clearance to even see."

"You seem to have gone to sleep on this one." Ignoring the tray and putting down his empty cup on the floor, Sir Anthony smirked. "He had to be removed before phase two began. We can't afford a loose cannon rocking the boat."

"On this memory stick," Kristina waved it around theatrically, reminding Claire of the final scene in a whodunnit, where all is revealed, and everyone gasps. If Kristina were hoping for something similar now, she would be disappointed. "Dr Pritchard stored every piece of information he discovered. Helpfully, he even included a summary document in which he drew all his conclusions together."

"He was quite the amateur detective." Leaning forward, slamming his hand on the table, Sir Anthony's face turned red again. "What he's got on there amounts to treason."

"There's no way we could let this reach the media." Finishing her coffee, Kristina placed the cup back on Claire's tray.

If they were expecting Claire to respond, they were disappointed. One question was flashing like neon in her mind. How did they discover this? It needed answering, but not yet. Something felt wrong. Only a scientist would understand any of Dr Pritchard's records, so who had they been in contact with? And for how long?

"Let's cut to the chase, here." Sir Anthony stood. More theatrics. "This memory stick is a copy. According to the tech boys there are three of these. Where are the others?"

"I have no idea."

"A controller with no control." Seeming to self-inflate, Sir Anthony looked delighted with his word play. Kristina gave no reaction, even when he looked at her. Claire said nothing. "Tonight's news will confirm that forensics believe he killed himself." Sir Anthony smiled. "Post-mortem results will be available in due course. We were unaware he had been suffering from depression, apparently brought on by death threats, of which we knew nothing. It is believed he took this course of action to protect his family." Sir Anthony paused. "I want you to give a fulsome tribute."

"That's fine."

"The Prime Minister and Leader of the Opposition will pay tribute in the House of Commons."

"What about Dr Pritchard's family?" Claire looked at the other two in turn. "There's a wife and two children."

"They won't be able to make any further statements, other than confirming they wish to be left to grieve in private."

"That's not what I meant, Anthony."

"They'll be taken care of." Sir Anthony stood, obviously eager to get away.

"How?" Claire also stood, positioning herself between him and the door.

"How what?" He let out an audible sigh.

"How will they be taken care of? What does that actually mean?"

"You don't need to worry about that." Claire shuddered as she felt Kristina's hand on her shoulder. "They'll be fine."

"It's well above your pay grade," Sir Anthony said. "Keep out of it."

"He was one of my staff." She spoke firmly. "I want to know what's going to happen to them."

"Need to know basis." His face reddened. "And you're not on the list. And never will be if I have anything to do with it."

"Who is on this list?" Taking a deep breath, Claire squared her shoulders. Staying calm took every ounce of her renowned self-control. She did not enjoy being bullied or ignored.

"That's confidential. And before you ask, you're not on that list either." Sir Anthony's idea of a joke fell way short of Claire's understanding of humour. "So, get out of the way. I've work to do." He didn't wait for Claire to move but pushed passed her. "Come on, Kristina, stop idling around. We're done here."

Sir Anthony strutted towards the door.

"Oh, by the way." Pausing, he turned back. "A team will be here any moment to search your property."

"I see." More theatricality, Claire felt.

Neither looked back as they left the house. Looking through her window, she watched a man approach them and open a car door. It wasn't someone she recognised. A new driver, probably.

Claire poured herself a large Jameson's, sighed and sat quietly for a few moments, wondering when Quinn would next be in contact. Her thoughts were disrupted by the doorbell ringing.

Day Three

Chapter 6

I

Having slept for a few hours, Adam made himself a mug of tea from the small supply provided by the hotel. He had finished all the coffee and supplies were only topped up in the mornings; at night there never seemed to be anyone on reception.

Notes

Once all our contracts were signed, the process moved rapidly from the planning to becoming operational. From the beginning there were regular injections, constant monitoring, numerous tests. We were all interviewed at the end of each day. Copious notes were taken. These must still be available as evidence. I remember the pain, the searing agony, as my body changed in response to treatment. At times it was almost unbearable, others were screaming, and I guess I was as well.

To begin with, only my appearance changed. Size, colour, face. Imagine your sense of self, of who you are, and of your place in the world confronted by such transformation. You can have no idea of how it feels to look in a mirror and see a stranger. It was like looking at a portrait in a gallery and trying to remember who they were. Looking for a label, or some biographical information. Nothing prepared me for this, you can't conceive of the shock I felt, even though we all knew what was coming. I've no idea how long I stood there just looking, trying to accept the swarthy face reflecting back was really me. I moved my arms and legs, they worked. I could hear and see. My mouth opened and closed without pain. There was nothing alien about the reflected image, but it just wasn't me and I was terrified. I didn't look at anyone else, so I can't say if they were all as spellbound as I was. I wanted to hear my voice but didn't dare speak for fear of how it would sound.

The oppressive silence was broken by cheering. Our trainers laughing and high fiving. Champagne corks popped like gun fire. More interviews followed, my voice sounding increasingly peculiar, rambling as I tried to focus. I was sweating, and at one point they restrained me with ropes. It got easier with each new identity, as curiosity replaced fear. But I never got over the anxiety of that first look, the fear of what would be facing me in the mirror.

My mind was one personality, my body another. This was not just like extensive cosmetic surgery. This was viciously schizophrenic.

It became easier when the mind became one with the body. Then all sense of your original self was hidden, and you became whatever identity they had chosen for you. More injections and you came back to yourself with little memory of what you'd been doing. Then, I found it was possible to shield part of my mind, to guard some memories, I really don't understand how, but it was exhausting. Some sense of importance made me write down my life up to that point and hide the papers. I thought it might make an autobiography when I became famous. The idea of celebrity was one of the buttons they pushed. Those pages are part of this document. Every word is true. I wrote down what was happening, probably not everything I had been doing, but all that I could remember. Then when I was myself, I read it. It was horrifying, so sickening that I can hardly bear to relate any of it here. But I must.

My first mission was to stir up anti-immigration feelings in an East London borough. You will probably have seen it in the media. Unemployment was high, and I pushed hard on foreigners taking jobs from the British. My body was stocky, with tattoos on both arms, and close-cropped hair. The TV news bulletins all focused on my speech, pundits discussed how angrily I'd spoken, how much hate came from my mouth. It was my rhetoric, they all agreed, that created the menace and hostile mood of the crowd, which then propelled them into action. There was a centre for asylum seekers in the next street and I led the chanting mass of demonstrators to the building. By now, there were no individuals, just a seething body of hatred. We chanted and threw rocks, planks of wood, anything we could get hold of. I provoked them to go further, it didn't take much. Then I organised a group to set fire to the building. Watch the footage, I'm right out front. People from inside ran screaming into the open, only to be set upon by dozens of 'my followers'. One man died trying to stop a woman being raped. A group of children were huddled together, trembling and sobbing. We beat them with clubs, telling them this country was not for them. They were not wanted. Two of the children were knifed, one died. I left the scene once the police started arriving.

Back in our headquarters, we all watched footage from my mission, alongside those of the others. The part of me I'd managed to shield was sickened, the reaction was so strong it overwhelmed my new identity. Others gloried in their successes, and they all cheered much louder at one operation. This was the death of a left-wing politician in Birmingham. We all saw the social media build up, created by my colleague; 'This MP is out of touch, she needs removing, let her go and live in fucking Syria. 'She is a traitor to our great nation.' And so on. It got thousands of 'likes' and a mob turned up at one of her public meetings. We saw on screen how they disrupted the meeting, how she tried to engage with the demonstrators, and asked them to meet her and talk through their grievances. I will never forget the last few frames as she was pierced through the heart by a crossbow bolt. The others all cheered. I just couldn't, but no one noticed, they were all too intoxicated by the violence. This was what the state wanted. It was embedded in us. There is a direct line from every riot to the people you elected.

Later, in my room, I wept. I punched myself. I regretted shielding part of my real identity. I hadn't been clever; it just tortured me and made every mission worse. My mind was scarred for life; there was this unbearable and permanent record I couldn't erase. However much I cursed myself, it made no difference, and I've come to believe this was my fate.

Why am I rebelling, you're probably asking yourself? Why not just keep going and avoid this fear of being hunted down? Abi. That's it. Abi and her values. How did we meet? Well, I was tasked with organising a violent campaign to disrupt a protest organised against fracking. Cheaper energy had been my mantra. My comrades went in with cans of petrol, intent on burning out the campaigners. As fires broke out and people ran, some in flames, Abi stood in front of me.

"How many pieces of silver are they paying you for this? How many deaths will be enough?" She wasn't scared, she was angry. Her green eyes blazed hotter than the fires. "I hope your paymasters in Westminster are proud of you. What's your name?"

"Adam." I answered without thinking because the question was so unexpected. Flames were close behind. I could feel the heat. People were screaming and running, their clothes ablaze. Abi remained still and stared at me.

"What happened to your humanity, Adam?"
She just turned and walked away.

That was it. I had to find her.

So, I'm holed up here in The Station Hotel. It may have been grand in the railway's heyday, but it's now just a ramshackle edifice, with steep, narrow stairs, peeling wallpaper, and sloping corridors. Room 8, where I'm staying, has a single bed from which my feet hang out at the bottom, a small rickety wardrobe leaning perilously to one side, and a portable television screwed into the wall, but seemingly on the brink of throwing itself to the floor. I never watch it as coverage of the riots is too painful. At night, the creaking and groaning leaves me terrified that the walls are moving slowly towards me, like in some cheap horror film. After dark, I daren't even make my way to the bathroom, four doors down the corridor to the left. I long for the sound of trains with their brakes squealing on the rails, then departing with an urgent rhythm, understandably intent on being somewhere else.

I tire easily, so I need regular breaks. I'm weary of working on this document. I had this idea that it will be important, that someone will read it, become outraged and talk to Dr Pritchard. Then it will all be stopped, the perpetrators held to account, but I might just be fooling myself. A Hollywood-style fantasy, with the superhero arriving just in time to save the day. Is that you? Maybe you won't care. Maybe you're happy to let Power do what it wants, provided you're connected, entertained, and getting enough sex? Can anyone be that apathetic? I hope not. I cling to the belief that people are inherently good and that what has been happening will disgust whoever reads this. Maybe one of my fellow guinea-pigs is also going down this route. I'd like to think so. But what if someone in power finds this document first? What an exercise in futility this would be then.

I try to stay optimistic, positive. But negativity worms its way through my confidence, finding gaps, slithering through the cracks in my mind. Fighting this is exhausting. The only thing I have left is the command, 'keep going'.

So, what would you do if you were me? How would you kill time while waiting to be unearthed like a fox on the run? It seems important to exercise. Not just for the physical benefits, but it's supposed to help with keeping positive. But it seems kind of futile. Will it help postpone the inevitable? Not really. When they find me, my level of fitness is hardly going to tip the balance in my favour. But I can't just sit and wait, and it does get me into the fresh air and out of this dingy room.

Walking at night delays facing the isolation of that room, the anxiety of incessantly checking the door is locked. My idea was to let the fresh air help tire me, but success in that direction has eluded me and I still don't sleep well. Maybe I should run, or mix it up a bit. Start walking, then run, then jog. Like those runners I see every night, with earphones presumably pumping their playlist as an encouragement. I reckon I use more energy just keeping out of their way, than on the rest of the walk.

Walking, rather than running, does allow me time to think. Well, that's the perfect example of a mixed blessing. The subject on my mind is always the same. Of course, it is. Tell me you'd be any different and I'll laugh in your face. If I can still laugh. So, I just wander around the narrow streets, trying to avoid the abbey that dominates every view in this town. Look up from the pavement, or shop window, and there it is. The spirit of Count Dracula and his blood lust oozes into the town, seeping into everything from the relentless parade of souvenir shops to the vulnerable and weak-minded tourists. It seems odd, me choosing this place as a bolthole. Whitby? Something must have struck a chord. A place from before, perhaps? Somewhere I enjoyed being, where I was happy. Perhaps I came here with someone, a close friend or lover. Perhaps we were like the couples I can see through the window, huddled together against the cold. And laughing. I see so many of them laughing. Why do they have to laugh? Whitby. The name rolls through my mind. Surely, it can't just be a random space. But I don't remember. My connection to this place remains a mystery, no matter how much I walk, look around, and think. It makes no difference. Every night brings the same dread, that those tracking me will know of the bond between this place and me. That they will come for me. I can't allow that. I need to see Abi again. To put things right.

Tonight, walking my normal route, with the usual spiteful wind coming off the sea and cutting through me like the hacking of a blunt razor blade, Abi's determined face engulfs my mind. She seems to be beckoning. So strong is this vision, I start to reach out to her, but grab only fists full of cold fresh air. She must be real, but she's not real. She seems to be there, but she's not there. I must get back to her. Making this document public will help; they won't dare stop me if all this becomes common knowledge. Will they? If I can't get back, for whatever reason, tell her this - that I didn't desert her, that I tried to come back, that I fucked it all up.

Tonight, about fifteen minutes into my walk, I felt a stone in my shoe. Moving over to lean against a shop wall and pulling off the shoe, I happened to glance back the way I'd come. The street lighting was dim, but there was quite clearly the figure of a man just standing in a shop doorway. His face was hidden, and his collar was turned up, but he didn't seem to be looking my way, so having replaced my shoe, I continued with my walk. A loose paving stone crunched underfoot and seconds later, I heard the same noise again. Pausing to glance in a shop window, where the light was better, I checked back and saw the same man, again not moving but this time staring in my direction. I turned, threaded through crowds of tourists and cut down an alley, then doubled back and began to run. Out of breath, back in my room, I stood for what seemed to be hours, staring through the window. My shadow was nowhere to be seen. Maybe it was just my imagination going into overdrive.

What if it wasn't? What if they've found me? What if… what if… It drives me mad. Whatever happens,

I want everything to come out. My greed, my stupidity, my crimes. For what? For money and the promise of fame. How could I have been so shallow? How could I not have noticed, not realised, the magnitude of what was happening?

I never believed in God, despite the best efforts of my mother, but now I pray. Can you understand that? I pray to a deity in which I have never believed, in the hope of Abi being kept safe. Secondly, if I have any remaining credit, I pray that these notes find their way into the hands of an independent and honourable individual.

Abi needs to know all this. I've left evidence for her to find. Photographs, phials of DNA. Get it analysed. Publish the results. Once she reads this, it will all make sense. Only then will there be a way back for me. And by you making it public, they won't be able to prevent our getting back together.

Except there's a man across the road, leaning in a shop doorway with his collar turned up. He's on the phone but looking towards the hotel. My plans need to change. I know they've found me, but it doesn't matter how. I need to get out of here now.

Day Three

Chapter Seven

I

Quinn sat in the only bar of The Adam and Eve.
Two men were playing pool further down to his left,
next to a door leading to the toilets. The pub
entrance was immediately to his right. A semi-
circular bar was in front, where several cask ales and
lagers were lined up lengthways. There were two
people serving, a young woman with a dazzling
smile and a young man in glasses, both wearing the
pub name on identical black tops. A seemingly
relentless tide of customers kept them busy, most
appearing to be regulars, leaving Quinn to wonder
what made eight-thirty on a Monday evening so
popular. Quiz night, he soon discovered as teams
began getting together, two groups tentatively
approaching him with offers of a place. Politely
declining, Quinn briefly wondered what in his
appearance made them think he would be a master
of trivia. He hardly watched TV, hadn't been to the

cinema for years and knew nothing about current affairs. Music, he knew. But there were hardly going to be many questions on that. Choosing a seat by the window from where he would be able to see Abi approaching, he sent a text telling her where he was sitting.

Finding her hadn't been difficult, Abi's name and photograph were easily found online and not just on social media. Quinn had found her on a website for climate change activists, she seemed to be highly thought of, as her posts were frequently supported by comments from many others. In the group's profile snapshot, Abi was one of five people in the foreground. Standing alongside her and recognized by Quinn from one of the photographs now sitting in his pocket, was the man everyone was looking for. The date was given as only ten days before, so Quinn reckoned there was a reasonable chance he was still in that identity. At least it was somewhere to start.

Locating Abi so easily, Quinn recognised, was a double-edged sword. If he could find her so quickly, then others wouldn't be far behind. How many and for exactly what purpose, he had no idea. But time wasn't on her side. Or his. How much should he tell her? All or nothing? Or somewhere in between. What could she cope with? He would have to play that by ear and trust his own judgement. But she had to give him something. Information. He needed that. A clue, a lead, some idea where Adam may have gone. Or why. However smart any investigator was, they all needed something to get them started, a plan to work with. And Quinn knew this was going to be a particularly difficult and dangerous case. Once again, he wondered who could possibly have recommended him.

Quinn's contemplations were interrupted as the quiz began with an explanation of the rules. Idly listening as prizes were announced, points and bonus marks explained, and penalty deductions described, it seemed more complicated than Quinn would have expected. The first round was announced, a picture round, bringing a mixture of cheers and jeers from the teams. As if on cue, as Quinn glanced through the window, he saw Abi walking purposefully towards the entrance.

His breathing quickened as he watched her enter the pub. She stood still for a moment, scanning the room, and then nodded to Quinn as he beckoned her across. Abi was not as tall as the image he had randomly created in his mind, but charisma surrounded her, attracting attention even to the extent of distracting customers from the quiz. Watching, and relieved by her lack of hesitation, which he took as proof she wasn't having second thoughts, Quinn waited for her to sit down.

"Hello, Abi, I'm Quinn. Pleased to meet you." Quickly trying to normalise a difficult situation, he held out his hand which Abi glanced at but ignored, folding her hands on her lap. Making eye contact was much more successful, if surprising. Quinn had expected suspicion, anxiety, maybe fear, but her wide green eyes radiated only self-possession and calm. Quinn took a few moments to re-set his expectations.

"Can I get you a drink?" Pushing on, Quinn was determined to avoid the risk of her leaving.

"Gin and tonic." She glanced back towards the door, Quinn deciding she was taking comfort from the short distance between herself and the exit.

"Large?"

"Please."

He queued at the bar, frequently glancing back to check she wasn't leaving, trying not to make it obvious. Experience told him that this was the most vulnerable time, the moment where people sometimes lost their nerve and chickened out. Relieved that Abi was displaying none of the danger signs for this, he watched her gazing confidently around, looking perfectly at ease, grinning at some of the quiz questions. Nevertheless, Quinn was taking no chances; he knew from previous encounters just how quickly such self-assurance could evaporate.

As usual, Quinn didn't queue for long; he had the knack in bars of being served quickly. Not as difficult a gift as is often believed, complimenting the staff and leaving 'a drink' for them upon arrival always worked. There were a few grumbles as the girl came straight over to him, but his most intimidating stare quietened the hubub. No one complained, even after he carried the drinks across and set them down on the table. Without speaking, Abi took a sip from her glass, as if immediately needing to confirm Quinn had brought her the correct drink.

As she raised her glass, Quinn noticed the sapphire ring on her finger. It wasn't ostentatious in any way, but stood out by being the only piece of jewellry Abi was wearing. Looks expensive, Quinn thought, the single blue stone surrounded by four small diamonds, and also important, as Abi continually toyed with it when her glass was on the table. If that tendency indicated her nervousness, it was the only sign he had seen since her arrival. More likely, it was just a habit. Whilst drinking, her attention remained fixed on him, her gaze sharp and piercing. This was no damsel in distress.

Quinn recalled their initial telephone conversation, when he had sensed her reluctance to meet him, and he had convinced himself that was a sign of uneasiness. It now seemed more likely that Abi was wondering if he were up to the job, or whether she should go it alone. Perhaps his assumptions had been flawed and this meeting was a reversal of those expectations. Could she be here to check him over, before deciding how useful he would be to her? Maybe, Quinn thought ruefully, he should have brought some character references along from whoever recommended him.

"So, Mr. Quinn. Do you have a first name?"

"I prefer just Quinn."

"Ah." She smiled and took another sip of her drink. "That embarrassing, is it?"

Smiling, he decided Abi was a woman well experienced with events happening and changing without warning; and assessing them, trusting herself to make decisions, then quickly adjusting to the new situation. And getting on with it. For a moment he wondered if this was going to make his job easier, or more difficult. Only time would tell.

"So, Adam's been gone five days." Pushing such thoughts to one side, Quinn decided to carry on as normal. Abi wasn't paying his wages. "Sometimes a man needs to get away. To cut loose. Kick out the jams. Isn't that what's happening here?"

"You're the detective." Abi gazed evenly at him and took another sip from her glass. "You tell me."

"I'm just gathering information at the moment, Abi." He tried a friendly smile. "I'm sure you wouldn't want me jumping to conclusions."

"Mr. Quinn, let me tell you what I know." Staring at him and setting down her glass, Abi made no attempt at returning his smile. "You've been employed to find Adam, but not by me. So, to my mind, that's at least two of us who don't believe he just needed to get away." Her voice hardened.

"Who's paying you, Mr. Quinn? And do they mean to harm him?"

"I can't answer that."

"Then why should I help you?"

Without replying, Quinn reached into his jacket pocket and pushed a photograph across the table.

"That him?"

"Yes, that's Adam." Abi glanced at the photo, then sat back in her seat. "I remember when it was taken. We were on a demo." Picking up the print, she studied it carefully. "It's not a great photo. You get no sense of the man."

"An accurate picture though?"

"Yes." Returning his gaze, she folded her arms.

The developing tension around their conversation was momentarily relieved by the crashing sound of glasses being dropped, followed by a raucous wave of cheers. Quinn noticed Abi had finished her drink but decided against getting her another. He was still worried she might take flight if the opportunity presented itself, not out of anxiety, but sheer cussedness.

"How long ago was this taken?"

"About two weeks ago"

"And he always looked like this?"

"Yes. Not always the same clothes, obviously." A frown appeared on her face, perhaps a moment of self-doubt. "That's a strange question."

"Really?" He slid the photograph back into his pocket.

"Yeah. The police asked the same question yesterday."

"The police?" Quinn felt a jolt.

"Yeah. You must've heard of them. Blue uniforms, suspicious minds, notebooks." Grinning, Abi's whole face lit up. "They came to see me."

For Quinn, at that moment, no one else existed. Her sense of humour should have lightened the atmosphere, and would have done, were it not for the icy feeling expanding inside his gut.

"You reported him missing?"

"No." A look of astonishment replaced her smile, making Quinn feel he'd broken some sacred creed, committed an unspeakable offence, and Abi's exaggerated sigh irritated him. "You really don't understand, do you? The police were always on the other side, they gave us no protection, but always supported the power. Most of us were isolated at least once from our groups and given what they called 'tough questioning'. Fists and boots don't listen to answers." She paused, her face flushed, eyes narrowed. "So, I would never go to them. Never. Adam wouldn't have wanted me to do that. He'd never forgive me."

Needing time to think, Quinn picked up Abi's glass and she nodded. At the bar, he heard the quiz results being announced, some good-natured accusations of cheating, and isolated cheers. Walking back to their table, he noticed Abi was looking towards the door, then checking her watch, before looking again.

"So, if you didn't report it, how did they know?"

"I don't know. They just turned up. No phone call or anything." Her words hit Quinn with the force of a physical attack. "How many of them?"

"Two." Staring at Abi, he noticed a slight hesitation for the first time. "I didn't tell them anything."

"You confirmed the photo was Adam."

"They already knew that."

"You saw their identification?" Watching her expression closely, Quinn saw nothing but confusion. She obviously had no idea a home visit to deal with a missing adult was almost unheard of these days, especially at such an early stage. And never if the person hadn't been reported missing. Glancing around the bar, Quinn could see no one taking any obvious interest in them. Now the quiz was over, customers were drifting away.

"I'm not stupid." Abi's fleeting glance towards the door was so brief, Quinn almost missed it. "I've been telling them fuck all for years." Grinning weakly, she downed most of her drink in one. "What's the problem?"

"Hopefully, nothing." Deciding he needed to get as much from Abi as he could in as short a time as possible, Quinn pushed on.

He quickly learned Adam had no family, at least not any Abi was aware of. No hobbies or interests, apart from their shared commitment to protesting about climate change. Adam had loved Buster, which Abi believed meant he wouldn't have left voluntarily. A sceptical Quinn ignored such romanticism but said nothing.

"How about money?" Quinn spoke urgently, looking for a reaction. "Was he flush? Did he pay for everything? Did he get you to sub him?"

"He never spoke about it."

"But did he seem to have enough? Or plenty? Did he count the pennies?" Quinn stared at her, hoping she would let slip some small bit of information that could help. "Or throw it around?"

"He was just... I don't know... normal." Another glance towards the door and then at her watch.

"Normal, generous? Or normal tight?"

"Cash. He always seemed to have cash."

"Not a card?"

"What does this have to do with anything?" Abruptly, Abi finished her drink. "He paid for stuff, I paid for stuff. Like normal. What do you do, check people are good for the bill before going anywhere? I bet you don't have many friends."

Deciding to move on, Quinn spread the now familiar images across the table.

"Do you recognize any of these other people?"

"No." She hardly glanced at the photos.

"I don't believe you." Quinn finished his drink. "Wake up and smell the coffee, Abi." Both barrels, he decided. "You need to get real here. This is not one of your sad little attempts to change the world." He leaned forward until he could feel her breath on his cheeks. "This is real life, the law of the jungle. It's nasty and could get nastier." Standing, he dropped his card on the table. "Get in touch when you grow up." Her arm reached out to prevent him leaving.

"Look." She also stood, jabbing her forefinger towards him. "I've been beaten up by police, by groups of thugs waiting in alleyways, by brainless morons paid by landowners. I get rape threats and death threats on social media. I don't scare easily." Real anger blazed from her eyes. "I just want to know he's OK. And why he left without saying anything."

"He's upset some powerful people, Abi." Quinn wanted to reach for her hand but decided against it. Her expression suggested she might just break his fingers. "I'm his only chance. Your only chance to find him."

"Why should I believe you?" She looked directly at Quinn. Then, once again, she glanced towards the door.

"Expecting someone?"

"I need the ladies." Looking around, she hurried away, knocking into a pool player on her way through. Quinn noticed the phone was in her hand by the time she reached the door. While waiting, he watched with amusement as the two pool players argued over whether the interference from "that clumsy bitch" warranted replaying the shot.

Sitting and thinking, Quinn recognised something had changed for Abi. Without warning, she'd become defensive and uneasy. Mention of the police? Not likely. She would have them for breakfast. And freeze the rest for later. Money? Maybe, but even that didn't ring true. Thinking back, it wasn't the subject that got to her, but the pile up of questions. The photographs? Much more likely, but why? That needed careful thought and a cautious approach. Did she or didn't she know about his alternative identities? It wasn't an easy question to ask.

Abi reappeared sooner than he expected; ignoring the abuse from around the pool table, she moved purposefully back to their table.

"You OK?"

"My friend." Abi replied immediately, her face flushed. "She was supposed to be here. And she's not answering her phone."

Abi had been expecting Sam. They had agreed earlier that she would join them, part way through the meeting, to give Abi time to assess Quinn and find out what he wanted. Sam was going to provide support, an objective view, a second opinion. It had been Sam's idea, she couldn't have forgotten, she never had before. Always they had been there for each other, forming a trusted support system whenever problems arose. Sam's job issues, Abi's debts, both of their issues with predatory men.

"Something must've happened."

"OK." Quinn seized her arm. "We go." He shoved her towards the door. "Now."

Surprisingly, Abi didn't object.

II

Half a mile away, in the warm bedroom, Sam turned on the light and looked at her watch.

"Shit." She checked a second time. "Shit." Her watch put the time at one hour later than the bedroom clock. It must be wrong. She seized her phone. Her watch was correct.

Jamie rolled over in the large bed and continued snoring. How he could get so tired after taking so little effort exasperated Sam. Flinging off the duvet, she leapt to the floor, cursing herself for not checking the time, for being there in the first place, for letting down Abi who had stressed the importance of her being on time.

Hunting around for her clothes, urgently discarded earlier and scattered around the bedroom, she frantically grabbed each piece, and hurriedly dressed, checking her watch in the hope of slowing time.

"Where are my sodding shoes?" She muttered under her breath, not wanting to wake Jamie, to face his questions, to lose her temper about his clock showing the wrong time.

"Shit. Come on." Running downstairs, Sam almost lost her footing trying to get into her coat. Pushing open the door, practically falling into the street, she struggled into her shoes. "Fuck." She looked left and right, frustrated by there being no other people in the street, so no chance of a lift. She ran towards the pub, her ankles twisting as her heels fought against her desire for speed. "Fuck's sake."

Throwing the shoes to the roadside, Sam ran barefoot along the pavement, swerving to avoid lamp posts and waste bins, still wondering about the bedroom clock. She was certain it had shown the correct time when they'd fallen into bed.

Through the bedroom window, Jamie Cousins grinned as he watched her leave, his investment secured. Some opportunities were just too good to miss.

"Cheers, babe. See you later." Checking his watch, Jamie retrieved a notebook from the bedside table and added this detail to previous notes. Who knew when this information would be valuable? Jamie believed strongly in insurance. He picked up his phone and clicked on a contact's name.

"Yes?"

"She's just left."

"Good. I'll transfer the agreed sum to your account now."

Lying back on the bed, Jamie threw the phone to one side and grinned. Changing the time on his bedroom clock had been a genius idea. Sam would soon learn the penalty for messing him about. She had been spending so much time with that no-good Abi, never telling him what they got up to. How many times had he told Sam that she needed to take care, that Abi was a control freak? That she was using Sam and it was destroying their own relationship, that it was affecting his desire to be intimate with her. Yet, she continued to spend entire evenings with Abi, flaunting their relationship, despite his clear warning that her job in the restaurant was at risk if she continued to ignore his opinion. All those secrets she kept, not wanting him to read her text messages, sometimes refusing to put her calls on speaker phone, even though he'd told her so many times that it was for her own good. To keep her safe. If she wasn't hiding anything, then what was her problem?

Well, Sam would find out tonight that he was right all along; his contact was going to hurt her, to teach her a lesson. Jamie had negotiated a substantial fee. Sam would come crawling back later, begging him to protect her.

He logged in to his bank account to confirm the transfer had taken place.

III

 At the same moment Jamie was online, a thin ruddy faced man at the far end of the pub finished his beer and moved towards the exit, unnoticed by either Abi or Quinn. He glanced towards them as he left, but they were too engrossed to notice. No one else paid him any special attention.

Weary from running, her legs aching, Sam walked as quickly as possible towards the pub. A voice cut through her breathlessness, from the car park; Sam was certain it was her name being called. She stopped and turned, her eyes searching through the dark, seeking out the owner of that voice. A strong hand clamped itself around her mouth, pulling her backwards.

Day Three

Chapter 8

I

Ending the call from Quinn, the Controller considered his update. Contact with the girl was a positive start, it was still early days, but his work so far was matching up with his reputation. On the negative side, his questions about any possible involvement from some foreign power, or other outside agency, were deeply troubling. Steering him away from such distractions, telling him to concentrate on the job he was being paid for, she wondered afterwards if it were possible? And if it were true, how could such a development have been kept from her? She had run this operation, step by step, from the beginning. Surely something would have stood out, attracted attention, raised the alarm. But as the possibilities began to nag at her, she realised it had to be taken seriously, as the potential consequences were almost unthinkable. If phase two were shared, the lives of every individual on the planet would be under government control.

Instructing her secretary that she was not to be disturbed under any circumstances, Claire thought back to the beginning of the operation. Going back to her detailed notes, she attempted to rule a line under each stage, before moving on, determined to find any weak point, any moment where disloyalty could have gained a foothold. She went through every report, training event, her own notes from meetings along with the minutes, checking the signatures of all agents and officials involved, reading and re-reading, scrutinising the personnel files for every individual involved at each point, but nothing was amiss. Approvals from the top floor matched every action. She checked the signatories for every document, there were no anomalies. Nothing had interfered with any of the missions carried out under this scheme. Online password security was watertight; Claire found no evidence or opportunity for hacking. No gaps in the timeline, no documents copied to others. No attempted access to the files by anyone else. She found nothing to suggest there had been any leaks, or the deliberate passing of information. But was it all too neat? Too clear-cut?

Opening Dr Pritchard's file and reading his reports, his doubts became clearer the more recent his research. Yet they were openly addressed. She decided to manually cross-reference all information, link together every step they had taken. But first, she needed a break to clear her mind. Guiltily cancelling her scheduled meeting with Sarah Pritchard, Claire decided to take a walk through the park, a practice she had fallen into when a serious matter needed thinking through carefully and without any distractions. Grabbing her coat, she dropped her phone into a desk drawer, which she locked before heading to the stairs. Avoiding lifts had become part of her most recent exercise regime, although she knew it would be no more successful than those preceding it. From an upstairs window, Kristina watched as Claire carefully crossed the road and entered the park.

Walking slowly, Claire considered the options.

One: Quinn could be wrong. In which case, fine. But her investigation would need to prove this.

Two: There was a mole in her department. Yet, data covering this operation was strictly controlled and no one, other than her, had access to all of it. She needed to see what was on Dr Pritchard's memory stick.

Three: The information was being passed by somebody further up the pay grades. In that event, all bets were off. Sir Anthony's comments about some facts being above her pay grade came to mind.

Considering each option separately, relating the facts she knew to each of them individually, then adding in the probabilities and possibilities, Claire compared the projected outcomes for each and their likely results on the project.

Almost two hours later, Claire returned to her office and locked the door. Most of the staff on her floor had left for the evening. There were sixteen voicemail messages waiting, but she listened to none of them. Her decision had been made and she was completely clear and focused on the path she intended to follow. Stopping this was her responsibility. There would be no distractions. She called the 'house-keepers', and had her office checked for listening devices. They found two.

A call to her opposite number at the American Embassy set up a meeting in the park, on the bench they always used.

II

It was a moonless night and Quinn drove quickly, constantly checking his rear-view mirror. Against his better judgement, he had given in to Abi's insistence on going to look for Sam. There was no sign of her at home, but Hero was sitting on the window ledge, staring out. He jumped down, wagging his tail at the sight of Abi and ran barking to the front door, but Quinn dragged her away. They moved on to the restaurant, where she wasn't on the rota and nobody had seen her that day.

"That's it." Quinn avoided looking at Abi. "No more fool's errands. We go." He pushed down hard on the gas and they sped away.

"You've got no lights on," Abi said, but Quinn didn't reply, his eyes searching out any potential threats. Multiple car horns blasted as they tore up a roundabout, tyres squealed as they took a left turn, seemingly on two wheels. Staring at him, Abi wondered if he were trying to intimidate her, and thought about mentioning the couple of police chases she had experienced. Both were much more frightening than this drive, with actual visible police cars in pursuit, flashing blue lights and sirens pumping up the pressure. Each time her composure in directing them through a route she knew had made certain her group avoided ending up in the back of a police van, staring back at several misogynist and tooled up officers.

Outside, the surroundings changed to narrow roads made tighter by parked cars down both sides, old Victorian houses divided into two and then two again. One car per house had become two or four, or more. Quinn dropped the car's speed, turned on the lights, and chose third gear.

"Ever thought about Formula One?" Abi grinned, her adrenaline still pumping. "Don't. Let's face it, your boy-racer days are long gone. Move on."

"I like to keep practicing just in case I ever get the call." He always got a buzz from putting his blue light training into practice but decided now was not the time for a discussion with Abi about advanced driving techniques.

"Where are we going?" As she spoke, Quinn glanced at her. Maybe she was acting. If so, she was the business; her composure went far beyond just the voice. She pointed through the window as they sped past. "I've been in that restaurant."

"Any good?"

"Overpriced. Small portions."

"There's a lot of that about. It pisses me off." Swerving to avoid a cat, Quinn clipped the side mirror of a parked car. "Whoops."

"Did you say where we're going?"

"Somewhere safe." Ignoring the lane markings, he forced the car alongside to let him turn right. Headlights flashed from behind, their car horn blasted three times, they moved within inches of Quinn's rear bumper. He took no notice.

"Safe for who?"

"Just safe." He let the steering wheel spin through his hands. The car behind had either dropped back or turned off.

Stopping at a red light, Quinn stared into his rear-view mirror and frowned. The black BMW behind them looked familiar, but he couldn't be sure. Better safe than sorry, he decided.

"Hold on." When the lights changed, he gunned the car forwards, then U-turned through a central reservation at the last second, before taking the wrong direction down a one-way street. They stopped near the end in a private parking area, Quinn watching the road until he was satisfied there were no threats.

"OK. It's fine." He answered a question that hadn't been asked.

"So, can we go now? I'd like to get to this place of safety before I wet myself."

"At your service, ma'am." Quinn gave a mock bow. "I aim to please."

"Why, thank you, sir. I'll recommend you to my friends." Abi smiled for the first time in a while. "And I'll be sure to tip you generously."

"I think we were being followed." He glanced towards her, not sure what he expected to see. Fear? Worry? Excitement, maybe. Abi showed none of those.

"Has anyone ever suggested you might be paranoid?"

"Abi, you need to start taking this seriously."
Driving slowly past his apartment block, scanning the streets and doorways, his eyes searched for anything unusual. A car parked out of place, a light shining from somewhere unfamiliar, a stranger staring around. Anything notable or remarkable. But he saw nothing out of the ordinary. A few lights were shining out from the apartments, a silhouette appeared briefly in one window, his own apartment was in darkness. He drove into a neighbour's parking space and stopped, figuring if anyone was interested in seeing if he were at home, it may delay them for a few minutes. "Keep your head down for a minute."

Another check around confirmed that nothing in the street stood out, everything was just as he expected it to be. The parked cars were all empty and there were no pedestrians hanging around. The twenty-four-hour convenience store seemed quieter than usual, but the staff were clearly visible and showing no signs of distress. A phrase came to mind, from a film he had seen, not that he could remember the title. 'I don't like it, it's too quiet' were the words he remembered. For the first time, they made sense.

It was this peaceful location that had attracted Quinn three years ago when he needed to find a place to live, his now ex-wife, Kay, remaining in the marital home. The divorce was amicable; at the time he'd no desire to challenge and no strength for confrontations. He wanted it over with. Quinn placed no blame on Kay. His nightmares kept them both from sleeping. Any future he had with the police was still up in the air, investigations were continuing, although he was still being paid. Kay tried hard to keep them together, he knew that. She made sure he went to counselling, suggested places they could visit, encouraged him to join her in exploring the local countryside. She couldn't have done any more. He rejected every suggestion, preferring scotch, and blues music. The rows became more frequent and hostile, starting with his reluctance to do anything, but quickly descending into randomly throwing about pure abuse. Eventually, Kay decided he was turning into someone she didn't recognise, or like, and reluctantly she gave up. Her solicitor issued divorce papers immediately upon receiving her instructions. Even then, Kay would have retracted every statement and withdrawn her action if Quinn had asked, but he didn't. For her, that was the last nail in the coffin of their marriage. He wouldn't fight for it.

"OK. We're here." Quinn pointed towards the block where he lived. "Wait by the entrance."

"That paranoia just keeps growing." Then, noticing his expression, she moved quickly away from the car.

Watching until she reached the entrance, Quinn checked around before joining her. Troubled by an indefinable feeling, he thought back over everything he'd seen or heard since they arrived. He had missed something, he knew it. Maybe a shape, some movement, or a sound. Quinn tried but found it impossible to pinpoint, though he had no doubt it was there. He had noticed it but subconsciously disregarded it as irrelevant. Move on, he told himself. It's too late, and much too distracting. He needed to forget it.

The door keys were in his hand as he arrived alongside Abi, and quickly opened the apartment block's entrance door. Once inside he breathed a sigh of relief. Neither spoke. Abi looked around the functional lobby, heard the lock click behind her, noticed the cold-looking concrete stairs to her left, and bleak-looking lift doors to her right. Graffiti was sprayed on the wall by the entrance.

"Follow me." Gently touching Abi's arm, Quinn moved to climb the stairs. "It's only one floor."

When they reached number 5, the door was ajar. Frowning, Quinn gently pushed it slightly further open and peered inside; there was nothing in the small entrance hall and the inner door was closed. With his left arm indicating Abi should stay back, Quinn stepped forward and cautiously pushed the door fully open. Some indistinct music drifted towards him from the next apartment, but despite there being no other sound, his left arm still told Abi not to follow. Warily, Quinn moved inside, out of Abi's sight.

III

Watching as he disappeared, Abi considered following him, but decided to wait. She inched forward and peered in to get a better view but could only see the hallway as Quinn had closed the inner door behind him. Impatiently she strained to hear the slightest sound, fighting against the feeling that she was becoming a spare part in some macho show of bravery. Before Adam had disappeared, any suggestion that she would have played second fiddle to a bloke she'd just met, would have creased her up with laughter. Then she would have mocked Quinn, instructed him not to be so melodramatic, and everything now seemed to exist on more than one level. She thought of Adam. Boyfriend, partner, lover, but what else? What of Sam, her only real friend, who had always been there when needed, but now wasn't anywhere to be found? And this man Quinn, apparently being paid by some mysterious third party to find Adam. What did they want with him? This was supposed to be a safe place, he had described it as exactly that, but had left her standing in this doorway while he checked it out. To Abi, that didn't suggest safety, rather the opposite. Where were they, anyway? Perhaps his manic driving hadn't been to get away from a following car but an attempt to obscure where he was taking her. Letting out a huge sigh, Abi frowned at the number of questions without answers. For the moment, she decided to trust her own instincts as always, and give Quinn the benefit of any doubt. After all, he'd left her here alone, giving ample opportunity for a get-away. That didn't really suggest a person intent on harming her. Checking her watch, she had no idea how long he had been gone. It seemed to be an hour but could only have been a couple of minutes. She decided to give it another two minutes before going in after him.

Then, without warning, Quinn re-appeared and stood in the doorway. For a moment Abi felt as though she was looking at a different person, his features were ashen, his movements erratic. He looked like he was rolling from a heavy-weight's punch to the head and longing for the knockout. She had seen a similar expression only once before, on the face of a man picked up by the other side during a demonstration. She never knew his name, but the image had lodged in her mind ever since. On automatic pilot, her mouth suddenly dry, Abi followed Quinn through the doorway and into the apartment.

Quinn gave her no warning, no advice to 'sit down', no 'prepare yourself', or 'something terrible has happened'. On the rare occasions this had happened to him before, he had felt such words only made things worse. Abi didn't agree, she felt it was unnecessarily cruel. In Quinn's defence, he had no idea the victim was Abi's friend.

It was Sam. Laid out on the floor, with little left of her face, her features beaten to a pulp. There was no sign of any weapon. Her arms were broken and both kneecaps had been smashed.

"Oh no." Abi gasped. "Oh God." She fell to her knees alongside the body. "No, no, no. Please God, no."

"You recognise her?" Quinn crouched beside her. "I'm sorry, I didn't…" Lifting his arms as if to give Abi a hug, he hesitated, then decided against it.

"Why? Who would do this?" Her shoulders began shaking, her face contorted. "It makes no sense." She refused to look away from her friend. "Oh, Sam, Sam."

"Best not move the body." Attempting to take control, Quinn didn't recognise his own voice. "Evidence." Again, he tried to console Abi; this time she pushed him away.

"Get off." She screamed. "Fuck off. Bastard. Leave me alone." Her tears came in uncontrollable sobs as she gently stroked Sam's hair. "This is all your fault." Her right arm flailed out at him, his chin taking a painful blow from her elbow. "Fuck off. It's my friend, I don't want you here." Almost wailing, Abi leaned over her friend, as if hoping for a miracle. "Who did this… who could…?" Her weeping drowned out any other words.

"Abi, please tell me who she is. You call her Sam. Who is she?"

Turning towards him, Abi's face was distorted with rage, her teeth bared. She grabbed for the first thing within reach. A cushion had fallen to the floor, Abi seized it and flung it towards him. "This is all your doing. Bastard. Your snooping around…. All those questions…. You made this happen." Now on all fours, she crawled towards Quinn, her eyes blazing. "It's Sam, you bastard. Sam. My friend." She grabbed the cushion again, pulled herself erect, and rained blows down on him. Quinn stood and took it, waiting for her to run out of steam. She fell back to the floor.

"It's Sam." She sobbed. "My friend. She was coming to the pub. I told you."

"Oh, Abi." Tears prevented her from seeing the shock registering on Quinn's face. "I don't know what to say. I'm so sorry."

"Sorry? You're sorry?" She moved back to kneel next to the body. "Stick your fake sympathy. I don't need it."

Moving away, Quinn looked again at the note he had found stuffed into Sam's mouth. 'Take this as a warning. You won't get another.' Abi did not need to see that.

"Why?" Wailing and banging her clenched fists into the floor, Abi then laid next to her friend's body. Side by side. "Why? Who would do this?" Silently watching her from the doorway, Quinn said nothing. He couldn't answer, couldn't even take a shot at it. There seemed to be no reason, other than pure evil, something he had begun to believe in during his recovery from the terror attack. He still fought against such a belief, but the horror occasionally overwhelmed him. Then he would drink. Since that dreadful night, Quinn had experienced this immediacy and level of pain on very few occasions but would never forget any of them. Every victim was etched in his memory, each were different, each tortured him uniquely from within. But this was in his apartment, his home. Where he'd had breakfast that morning, watched television the previous night. Where it should be safe. Was this the reason Sam's death seemed so traumatic? Or was it just the scale of violence used, far beyond what would be necessary?

"I've called the police." Quinn remained by the doorway, speaking quietly. Abi gave no sign of hearing him but kept whispering to her friend and tenderly stroking her hair. He felt in awe of Abi's strength of character, moved by the intensity of her love and compassion. His own first reaction had been to run to the bathroom and throw up. Turning away, feeling ashamed, he moved to the window, and looked for any signs of the police arriving. What he saw in the shop doorway opposite, though, were two pedestrians in dark coats, collars turned up, staring at him. There was no mistaking where they were looking. When the sirens sounded, one gave a little wave and they strolled away.

"We'll find the bastards who did this."
Turning towards Abi, Quinn spoke softly, but
urgently. "I promise."

"Promise. Hah. Yeah." Almost snarling, she
spun around and glared. "Easy to say, mister no first
name."

"We want the same things, Abi. We want to
find who did this. For Sam."

"Don't you use that name." Screaming, she
came at him with flailing fists, tears streaming down
her cheeks. "Never use that name. You have no
right."

Grabbing both her wrists, Quinn held them until the
rage subsided and she buried her face in his chest.
Stroking her hair, this killing began to feel personal.
That was not good.   "We must do this. You and
me." Gently lifting her face, he stared into her eyes.
"Find whoever did this and lock them away
forever."

Before she could reply, there was a loud knock at the door. Startled, Abi pulled away and stared at him with narrowed eyes.

"Open up. Police."

"It's OK, Abi." He held her as she tried to move towards the door.

After checking through the eye hole, Quinn let them in.

Within seconds the apartment filled with uniforms, forensics, detectives, all of whom wanted Quinn and Abi to be somewhere else. Anywhere else, just so long as it was out of their way. For Abi, everything seemed to move in slow motion; she wanted this drawn-out process over with, and craved answers. What sort of human could inflict such horrific injuries? The pain Sam must have endured, Abi couldn't bear thinking about. Yet, that was the question that would not go away. She could hear Sam's voice begging for mercy, pleading for some basic human compassion. How many beatings did she take before falling into unconsciousness? Abi prayed it would be few. Now she wanted to be some place as far from all this as possible, preferably not with Quinn. The police officers had other ideas, their favourite being a trip to the police station. Abi pleaded they couldn't believe she had anything to do with this. Quinn vociferously protested, quoting criminal law, the right to a solicitor and anything else he could throw into the mix.

Detective Chief Inspector Barnard arrived with his sergeant, George Baker, from The Singing Detectives. Relieved to see a friendly face, Quinn waited with his arm around Abi, hoping George would come over. The two officers were physically opposites. Barnard was shorter, moved around slowly, always with an air of resignation hanging over him and always sported a trilby when away from the station. His sergeant, George, was about ten years younger, taller well-built, with a face shaped like a coffin. Barnard reached Quinn and Abi first.

"Mr Quinn, is it? He didn't wait for a reply. "This your flat, sir?"

"It's my apartment, yes."

"Mmm. Nice." He glanced around, more for effect than out of interest, Quinn felt. "Lived here long, have you?"

"Three years."

"And who's the young lady?" Opening a packet of mints. He slipped one into his mouth.

"My name's Abi." Glaring at Barnard. Abi pulled away from Quinn. "You can talk to me directly, you know. I am an adult."

Quinn tried not to smile, but noticed her comment had no effect on the inspector's expression. It was a positive sign, though; Abi seemed to be recovering herself.

"Yes, well. I can see that." Turning, he beckoned his sergeant across. "George, Get their statements."

"Sir."

They left nothing out, other than the involvement of the security services. If Abi was surprised to hear Quinn talking about how she had hired him to find her boyfriend, she gave no indication. Giving her statement afterwards, she backed this up.

"Thanks, Abi."

"I'd rather be dealing with you, than them." Smiling weakly, she looked him in the eye. "Besides, I don't know who's paying you." Quinn guessed this small deception had given her something other than Sam to occupy her mind. Both stood watching as George spoke to the Inspector. "And you now owe me a favour."

"I've put my neck on the line here." George spoke quietly, nodding his head towards Barnard. "You obviously can't stay here, so he's agreed you can both head over to her house." Checking around, he leaned forward and dropped his voice. "There'll be a constable outside the door. He won't seek to gain entry unless he suspects something."

"Thanks, George."

"Look, mate, be careful. I know you." Again, he glanced around, before gently leading Quinn out of Abi's earshot. "If you're thinking of running around doing detective stuff, don't take too long over it. If the boss finds out you've been out and about, he'll go off on one." George grinned. "Maybe more than one."

"Look, George." Nodding in response to the sergeant's advice, Quinn spoke quietly. "I know it's early days, but is there anything you can tell me about how she died?"

"You didn't hear this from me."

"I know the deal."

"Whoever did it, they didn't just want to kill her." Pausing, they both glanced towards Abi, who was leaning limply against the wall and staring at the floor. "Is she alright? Does she need a doctor?"

"She'll be fine." Knowing he only had a little time, Quinn's voice lowered but its urgency increased. "Tell me."

"They wanted her to suffer." George took a deep breath. "First impressions, mate, but she wouldn't have died quickly." Quinn felt his legs go weak, and held on to a chair back, not wanting to fall. "As far as we can tell, it wasn't a robbery. Her cards and cash are still in her purse. Plenty of ID as well."

"Any idea about the time of death?"

"Can't be sure yet. An hour maybe, two tops."

"Thanks, George. I owe you."

"Yeah. A nice long drum solo."

They moved back towards Abi, who pushed herself upright as she saw them approaching.

Finishing the inspector's list of conditions, George told them to stay together. Abi sighed as she saw him winking. A detective would be with them shortly for further questioning.

"I reckon you've got an hour tops," George murmured. And no, Quinn could take nothing from his flat until the scene of crime officers had finished. "So, no pyjamas."

"We'll get off now." Sensing Abi was about to offer a reply to George's innuendo, Quinn steered her towards the exit.

"Quinn? Mmm. I know that name from somewhere." Barnard smiled as they walked past. "Don't leave town, will you."

Outside, the media were already gathering, sensing blood. Vultures looking for a carcass to feed on. Their shouted questions and pleas for photos gave Quinn no time to wonder who had supplied their tip off. That would have to wait. Grabbing Abi's hand, he pulled her along as they shoved their way through to his car.

They drove to Abi's house in silence, apart from her directions, and it was a much calmer experience than the previous journey.

As Abi opened the door, Quinn watched Buster careering towards her, his tail like helicopter blades in full flight."

"That sergeant. A mate of yours?"

"We know each other, yes."

"Spends a lot of time watching cop series from the seventies, does he?"

"Don't let that fool you. He's sharp."

Buster was now on Abi's lap, dividing his time between gazing adoringly at her, and licking every uncovered piece of skin he could find.

"Can I use your toilet?"

Abi pointed up the stairs without looking at him.

"Door on the left," was all she said.

Washing his hands, he glanced in the mirror and saw his father's face mocking him as always. 'You're out of your depth,' the apparition seemed to be saying. 'You've nothing to go on.' Then his big finish, his all-time favourite encore. 'You've always been weak. You should be more like your brother. Now, he would have had this sorted already.'

"Just when I thought things couldn't get worse," Quinn muttered to himself. "You show up."

Turning away, he briefly considered phoning Will to check on the old man but couldn't face the inevitable argument. Will was confrontational at the best of times, and this was far from that. Instead, he phoned the Controller with his latest update, keeping it brief, reluctant to encourage any questions.

"You tell the police nothing." Her voice was cold, with no mention of sadness about Sam's death. "As you will remember, you're bound by The Official Secrets Act."

"How could I forget."

"And you make sure the girl plays ball."

Quinn controlled his desire to laugh. Only someone who had never met Abi could make such a demand.

"We need to get into Sam's house." Abi was standing up as he returned, still wearing her coat and scarf. "Before anyone else."

"I don't think so." Sitting down, Quinn tried to sound authoritative. "You heard what George said."

"I heard he said we had about an hour. That's enough time."

"Why Sam's house?"

"I'll tell you on the way." Pacing around, Abi even ignored the remains of a soft toy Buster laid at her feet. Its importance to the dog was clear from the difficulty Quinn had in identifying any original features. "Don't you understand?" Her words came at speed. "We mustn't waste time."

"Well, time is one thing I've plenty of." Stretching out his legs, Quinn smiled. "Got any scotch? I could really use a shot."

"No. He said one hour, tops." Grabbing at him, she frantically pulled at his arms, then   pushed at the chair from behind, anything to get him out of his seat. "We need to go now." Finally, hands on hips, fury pouring out of every inch of her body, Abi stopped. "Right then, mister 'look after your own skin Quinn', I'll go on my own."

"Wait." Standing, Quinn manoeuvred himself between Abi and the back door. "Just talk to me. I'm trying to help but I have no idea what's going on in your head. For all I know, you're leading me into a trap. And I'm kind of committed to staying alive. It might not be much of a life, but it's all I've got."

"You're getting paranoid again." She almost smiled, but her eyes were scowling.

"Look, I'm on your side. You need to start being open and honest with me."

"I've remembered something." Abi stared at him, and on her face he saw the protester, the campaigner, a person with no concern for how the odds were stacked, ready to take on the world, bursting with the certainty that right was on her side and it would prevail. "I think it's important and we need to get to it first."

"And this 'something' is at Sam's?"

"Yes." Quinn felt Abi's stare piercing through to his essence, a silent questioning. Could she trust him? Would he stand alongside her, back her up, if things got tough? Or run? Could she see the terror attack? His response to horrific danger? Seconds turned into minutes, then longer still until she switched off the stare. Crunch time, he realised. Now was the moment it would go one way or the other. He was either in, or out.

"Sam thought it was significant." Finally speaking, Abi seemed to be satisfied. "We found it when we went through Adam's things. Sam said we should move it somewhere safe."

"So, it's something physical and it's at her place?"

"Yes. It's four phials of liquid."

"But you don't know anything else?" He felt his skin start to crawl.

"No. We found it with Adam's stuff. Refrigerated."

"Could Sam have told her attacker about this?" Quinn frowned as he remembered George's words 'they wanted her to suffer'. Maybe, they wanted information.

"You think this is part of why Adam disappeared?"

"I don't know, but I think we need to proceed in the belief that it is."

"Then we need to get over there."

"If it was part of Adam's possessions, then it's likely to be important." Speaking slowly, Quinn picked his way through the possibilities. It depended on whether Sam recognised the importance of these phials. If she did, and told them, it could already be too late. "Were there any labels? Any information?"

"Nothing." Abi's restless eyes were focused on Quinn, waiting for his response.

He wasn't letting her go alone, that was certain, so the decision made itself.

"OK. How far?" Quinn moved towards the door.

"A five minute walk."

"You've got a key?"

"Yes."

"Then, let's go." They left through the garden and along an unmade footpath. The police constable standing by the front door had no idea they had left.

Stopping outside Sam's front door, Quinn listened but heard no movement from inside. The place was in darkness. Putting his finger to his lips, he slowly turned the key and gently pushed the door open. What seemed to be a whirlwind rushed past; instinct drove Quinn to side-step and drop to his knees, feeling a physical and tangible force. For a split second, he froze. Blood pounded in his ears. An explosion, screams and panic detonated into his mind. Sweat ran down his body. He wanted to run, but he didn't. It wasn't a repeat, it was just Hero bounding towards Abi, standing on his hind legs, paws on her waist.

Quinn exhaled his pent-up breath, cheeks puffed out; it felt less like a sigh of relief than a tidal wave engulfing his entire body. Leaning against the wall as his knees almost gave way, Quinn closed his eyes and waited for his heart to stop pounding, half-expecting it to burst through his chest at any moment. Then, silent laughter racked his body. It was just a dog. A friendly dog, one that recognised Abi and was obviously delighted to see her. Hero. Great name, difficult to live up to, but Quinn would give him every treat in the house for being himself. And not a killer. Recovering his composure, Quinn realised Hero's behaviour did signify one important fact. It was unlikely there were any intruders in the house.

Looking around, he saw the stairs were directly in front of him, with a closed door to the right and, on the left, a curved archway apparently leading to a small kitchen, from where Hero had appeared. Cautiously, Quinn moved right and pushed open the door, as Abi forced her way past him, fists clenched. She gave the impression of hoping to find an intruder, eager to get the release of kicking the shit out of someone. Anyone. However big and powerful they were. Whatever weapons they had to hand, Quinn's money would be on Abi. No contest.

Following her into the room, he snatched her hand away from the light switch, flinching as she jerked her head around and pushed her face inches away from his. Given the choice between Abi in this frame of mind and facing an angry wolf, Quinn would choose the wolf. A whole pack, even. Pointing to his phone, Quinn flicked on its torch. The room seemed undisturbed.

"Where are the phials?"

"Upstairs." Pointing her finger upwards with an unnecessarily violent jab, Abi pushed past him again and stormed up to the landing. Quinn followed, more carefully, trying not to make any noise, despite realising it was pointless after Abi's whirlwind impression. Even so, each creak from the stairs reached Quinn's ears like an alarm being sounded. At the top, Abi was already in one of the three rooms.

"In here." Kneeling, Abi was reaching into a small beer-fridge in the corner.

Pulling out a plastic container, she opened it and checked inside. "Here," she said. "They're still here." For the first time he noticed the silent tears running down her face. "They must be important."

Checking around the room, Quinn sighed and shook his head slightly, irritated by her having switched on a bedside lamp. He noticed the unmade bed and clothes strewn across the floor, the closed curtains, the laptop on the floor, still plugged in. Nothing seemed to be out of the ordinary, judging by Abi's lack of concern.

Finding her composure astonishing, Quinn wondered if he would be as strong in her position. Hadn't he almost gone into a full-blown panic attack, just because of a friendly dog? Yet, here was Abi in the house of her murdered friend, in the bedroom where she slept, showing no signs of distress. He watched as Abi paused to look around, obviously determined to remember every single detail. The underwear drawer half-open, the pyjamas on the floor by her bed. A book laying open on one of the pillows. An empty CD holder, 'Kind of Blue' by Miles Davis. Finding the disc itself, Abi slotted it back into the holder before sliding it into her pocket.

"A memory," is all she said. Quinn had hardly noticed a calm Hero sitting alongside Abi, intent on going nowhere else, just staring at her face.

Moving downstairs and replying to Quinn's question, Abi told him there was nothing else she wanted to take from the house.

"I'm bringing Hero, though." She didn't wait for a reply. "He's not going to a rescue centre. I'll look after him." Quinn decided against arguing. What would be the point?

"Try and keep him quiet," he said.

Arriving back at Abi's, entering the same way they had left, Quinn checked around.

"It seems we got lucky," he reported to Abi, wanting her to understand how fortunate they'd been. The uniformed officer was still there, but there were no signs of any other police having turned up yet. Checking his watch, they'd been gone forty minutes.

Buster's adoring welcome more than matched Hero's earlier. Watching them chasing each other, playfighting over a length of cord, each pulling from opposite ends, for the first time Quinn got why people had dogs.

"Tea?" Watching Abi joining in with Buster and Hero, he decided to make himself useful.

"Gin."

"We should lay off the booze until the cops have finished with us. We'll need a clear head."

"OK." Not for a second did she drag her attention away from the dogs. Quinn shrugged and moved into the small kitchen. Looking around, he lifted two mugs from the sink, both adorned with the slogan, 'Stop Talking. Do something. Save The Planet'.

After inspecting and sniffing them, he rinsed both under the hot tap and then filled the kettle.

It was one of those moments, bringing a sense of every act being important, like a performance that needed to be remembered in the minutest detail. A rehearsal. Then every detail could be recounted later, maybe even if questioned, needing a justification for every action, however slight. Even mundane movements, like taking the milk from the fridge, took on a significance far beyond their habitual routine. To Quinn, every second seemed critical.

"Milk?" he called. "Sugar?"

"Just milk." Abi responded only when Quinn leaned his head round the door to check she hadn't scarpered. She was hugging Buster and speaking softly, perhaps for her own comfort and looking nowhere else.

The kettle did its work, bubbling and hissing as its duty was completed. Quinn returned with the two mugs and watched as Abi stared into hers, as if searching for something.

Buster looked at Quinn uncertainly. He looked back towards Abi, who smiled and nodded. He jumped down and cautiously started to sniff around Quinn, his tail still wagging, if much more slowly. Quinn said nothing but offered his hand for Buster to sniff, hoping the silence would pressure Abi into talking. When she did, it was not at all what he was hoping for.

"I think I'll keep Hero." Her blank stare gave nothing away. "What do you think?"

"I don't give a…." Controlling himself with some difficulty, Quinn stared at Abi. "What planet are you on?"

"Oh, good question, Ace." She slowly clapped her hands. "Often use that as an opener, do you?"

Despite himself, Quinn smiled.

"Normally only with aliens."

"Do I look like an alien?" Deliberately, Abi widened her eyes and gave a coquettish smile.

"No, you look like…" Quinn turned away, feeling suddenly hot, moving to the window, and closing the curtains. "Maybe you should think about your boyfriend and the trouble he's in."

"Maybe I've had too much reality lately." She spoke softly, her slender fingers still cradling the empty mug. "Perhaps I just need to escape it for a while."

"It won't go away."

"Yeah." She sighed. "I know."

"You've been holding out on me." Taking a deep breath, Quinn sat as far away from her as was possible in the small room. He felt angry, close to losing control, but confused about why. His voice hardened, becoming unsympathetic, on the edge of being cruel. "Your friend is dead. Whoever killed her intends you to be next and I'm no hero. I'm not getting between you and them." Leaning forward, Quinn struggled to find the words he wanted. Abi raised her eyes to meet his, holding her gaze steady, keeping his eyes captive. Finally, she placed her empty mug on the floor. Neither spoke and the silence became deafening; his own breathing was all Quinn could hear.

"You're a fool, Ace." Abi broke the silence and spoke softly, without malice.

"I've been called that before." Freed from her stare, Quinn felt the hit.

"That's hardly reassuring," Abi said slowly. "You always have a lot to say, Mr. Quinn." Lifting

Buster on to her lap, she left Hero stretched out by the side of her chair. "But are you able to listen?"

"Try me."

"Those documents you showed me, I have seen them before. But only after Adam left."

"I don't believe you."

Abi reddened, turned her face away and looked around the room.

"I'm getting pretty pissed off with you." She spoke quietly, but with a harder tone. "The fact remains that it's true. And that what you believe is irrelevant."

"Don't stop now, Abi. Let's have both barrels." If she wanted to talk, he decided to go with it.

"Has it occurred to you that we really know nothing about other people, even those closest to us?" Abi gently placed Buster on the floor, slowly stroking his back, then stood and began to pace around. "Or are you so fucked up by the system that you believe in those meaningless absolutes, good and bad? One or the other, with nothing in between? God versus the devil? Is that it?" Ignoring his earlier instructions, she poured herself a gin. "In your line of work, you must've come across dozens of examples to prove that is a load of shit. Life isn't that simple." She turned and added tonic, either as an afterthought, or because neat gin didn't do it for her. "Couples that've been together decades, yet one decides to kill the other; bank managers, pillars of the community for years, discovered to have been embezzling their employers; devout Priests abusing children in their care."

"OK. OK." Quinn held up his hands in surrender. "So, we don't really even know our best friends."

"Yes. That's what I'm trying to get you to understand." Becoming animated, Abi raised her voice and began to gesture with her arms, spilling her drink without noticing. "Why is it so difficult for you to get your head around one thing? I had no idea about any of this, I still don't know what 'this' is.

Mr Quinn, Adam was my boyfriend. I hadn't known him for long, but he was funny and kind. He was obviously something else as well. I really need to know what that 'something else' was. Or how do I make sense of that relationship, those months, the things we did?"

Unable to answer, Quinn picked up the two empty mugs and returned them to the kitchen. He felt not just the sense of what she said, but was also convinced by the passion with which she spoke. Leaning forward over the worktop and staring through the window into the dark, he tried to nail down something tangible from the maelstrom swirling around in his mind. Connections came together and flew apart. The Controller, those phials of liquid, Sam's murder.

He opened the fridge and stared at the phials. Something the Controller had said to him hovered at the edge of his memory, but he couldn't pin it down.

Only one thing was certain, he had a decision to make. Once made, there would be no going back.

"So, Mr. Quinn. Still not going to tell me your first name?" A calmer Abi grinned as he came back into the room.

"Maybe, when we get to know each other better."

"That must be some really embarrassing name." She stroked her chin. "Shall I have a guess?"

"Got any scotch?"

"I thought we were keeping our heads clear until the cops had finished kicking the shit out of us."

"Well, I need to catch up with you. Anyway, they'll be here soon." His watch showed it was almost an hour since they'd got back from Sam's.

"Not in any great hurry, are they?" Smiling, Abi crossed the room, brushing her arm against him as she headed for the alcohol. "Scotch," she announced triumphantly, holding the bottle in the air. "And more gin for me."

IV

Cradling a large twelve-year-old malt in his hand, Quinn stood the bottle down by his chair and looked at Abi, wondering if they were both thinking the same things. What was in those phials? Do we tell the cops about them? They must be linked to the whole genetic engineering process, but in what way he had no idea. Neither could he decide how to go about finding out. Maybe when he next updated the Controller, he could ask what she knew. Demand answers. Maybe. He held out little hope; secrets were her bread and butter. More immediately, though, how much did Abi know? Was she holding out on him? Trying to protect Adam? In any event, there was no point talking to the police about it. Genetic engineering? One person physically changing colour or gender? Quinn could just hear their comments.

"That must be some strong stuff you're on."

"You need to take it easy or it'll be space-ships next."

And so on. It would just be a joke. Or they would believe the entire situation was part of some elaborate sexual fantasy, with Sam's killing just an extension of that. The Carver case came to mind. They were a married couple who sought out young men and women for their own twisted gratification, their needs intensifying until only killing quenched their desires.   "Nice scotch." Quinn raised his glass in Abi's direction.

"Adam liked it. I can't stand the stuff."

"It's an acquired taste."

"I'll take your word for it." Sipping her gin, she kept her eyes on him. "So, Mr. no first name Quinn, what's this all about?"

How much could he tell her? He was no closer to answering the question he faced when they first met. Maybe that was the wrong question. How much could she take? Would that be better? Hardened, as she obviously was, by demonstrations and protests, this was different. It wasn't about the planet or carbon emissions, or whatever else she wanted to challenge, this was personal. Direct and dangerous. Her friend's violent murder, her boyfriend's disappearance, both must have pushed her to the limit. So how would she react if he told her what Adam was really doing? Everyone had limits. Despite her resolve and obvious strength of mind, just one small damning fact revealed at the wrong time, and she would be devastated. A train-wreck. He couldn't even be sure how much of what he had been told was relevant, or even true. There were many questions, but very few answers. Events were moving so fast that, whenever he seemed to be getting on top of one thing, other issues bulldozed their way in. Not just individually, but in battalions. He would need to take her fully into his confidence at some point, Quinn realised, and just hoped he would recognise the right moment when it came along. If it did.

Abi, though, was obviously not ready to give in, and it was apparent she was becoming impatient.

"Don't you trust me, Mr. Quinn? Is that what it is?"

"Yeah. That's what it is." He hadn't wanted to say it, hated doing so, but there was no other answer he could give without coming clean about everything he knew.

"Then we know where we stand. I don't trust you either." Smiling, Abi raised her glass in mock salute. "But I think you need me more than I need you."

That smile seemed to cut him in two.

"And why would that be?"

"Work it out, Ace." She put Buster on the floor, his eyes following her every step as she stood and poured more gin into her glass. "You don't mind me calling you Ace, do you? I forgot to ask. I just find first names more friendly, making people easier to trust."

"Please yourself." Quinn's attempt at indifference fell flat; he knew it and so did Abi.

"I will." Her eyes moved up and down his face. "Who killed Sam. And why?"

"At a guess, I'd say someone wants to get at you." Abi's ability to focus and tackle events head-on astonished Quinn. She would bludgeon her way to the truth, browbeating any person getting in her way. He needed to get rid of the idea she was vulnerable in some way. It struck him hard that she would never have run away that night, as he did.

"This is all to do with Adam, yes?" She kept her eyes on his face.

"Most likely." His gaze dropped to the glass of whisky.

"So why not kill me?"

"It wouldn't get them anywhere." Quinn decided she deserved some of the truth and could probably deal with it better than him. "They're putting the frighteners on. They think you know where your boyfriend is. Killing Sam is like a final demand."

"Don't sugar-coat it, will you?" She raised her glass and smiled grimly. "Anyone ever say you have a way with words, Ace?"

"Yeah. It's a gift."

"And all this is to do with those documents?"

"Yep. Those documents you claim to know nothing about." Quinn poured more scotch. "Let's get real here. This is not some protest march, where you might get arrested and roughed up a bit. That would be a walk in the park compared to this. Do you understand? Your friend is dead, and I wouldn't bet against you being next on the list."

"Your bedside manner needs a bit of work, Ace."

"Is that all you can say?" Quinn took a deep breath; her indifference needed puncturing. "You need to realise that to these people you're nothing. A fly to swat. Virtually invisible without a magnifying glass." He leaned forward. "They wouldn't notice if they stood on you, until they decided to scrape you off their shoes."

"And you're the great knight on his big white horse, come to rescue me. Is that it?"

"Whatever you believe." Quinn finished his drink, angry with himself for opening-up this can of worms. "I'm all you've got."

"Who's paying you to find Adam?" Abi's resolve flashed across her face, igniting an almost physical manifestation of determination.

"I can't tell you that." Quinn resisted the extraordinary force of her expression only by turning away. "My employer wishes to remain anonymous."

"Secrets and lies. You seem to like them. No first name, no information." Abi's voice was cold and expressionless. "A man of mystery who expects me to tell everything but offers nothing in return."

"I have a living to earn."

"Well, there it is." She laughed bitterly. "The 'just following orders' get out." Another snort of unpleasant and derisive laughter. "How did I know that was coming?"

Saying nothing, Quinn wrestled over whether this was the moment, the right time to tell her everything he knew. She deserved the truth, to have the information he had, that much was clear.

"I told you about the phials." Abi rounded on him furiously. "I didn't need to. I even went with you to get them. I've been upfront and straight with you, so you can fucking well tell me what's going on."

"That's not how this stuff works." Quinn stared directly into her uncompromising green eyes and felt a sudden and unexpected surge of desire.

She sat silently, just staring at him. A long minute went by.

"I hate people like you." Abi eventually spoke. "You think anything you decide to do is fine, whatever effect it has on others. That you can just use people to suit yourself and give nothing back."

"Listen, we're both on the same side." Quinn stretched out his arms, palms upward. "We both want the same thing."

"Don't treat me like an idiot, Mr. Quinn." That bitter laugh again, more hostile this time. "I want you out of my house."

"Are you going to tell the uniform outside your front door?" It was an effort, but Quinn kept his voice calm. "The one making sure neither of us leaves?"

"Are you going to tell me what those photos and documents are about?"

"I can't."

"Frightened of getting into trouble, Ace?" Abi poured more gin, her hand showing no signs of shaking.

He remembered being sneered at before, but never so effectively.

"Company man, are you, Ace? Always do as you're told, do you? Keep your nose clean, never upset the authorities?" Her ever-increasing mocking laughter cut right through him. "Like they give a shit about you." Desperate to defend himself, Quinn had no idea how to deal with Abi. He wanted to tell her she was wrong, to recount all the times he had backed the individual against authority, but the words had vanished. Abi had no such problem and hadn't finished with him. "Yes sir, no sir. Is that how it is?" Her scorn did the trick.

"OK, Abi." Almost without realising, he slowly began to talk, then more quickly, carefully explaining the information he'd been given about Adam. Showing no reaction, Abi sat and listened impassively, but never once moved her gaze away from his face. When he had finished, he looked for Abi's reaction, as an overwhelming sense of relief flooded through his body. Why had he not done this sooner?

"We must find him and help him." Abi hadn't moved, she appeared calm, which Quinn found astonishing. "Or are you, Mr. Ace, going to hand him over to the secret police?"

Having not thought any of this through, not given any consideration to his contract with the state, Quinn struggled to find a reply.

He was saved by a loud knock at the door.

Day Four

Chapter 9

I

Jamie was watching the local news on television. Not intentionally, as his interest in current affairs sat somewhere between complete indifference and total dislike. His one exception was the current round of riots, showing nightly on the national news, allowing him to fully enjoy the filmed violence, without needing to think about the cause. That isn't to say he was ill-informed. Jamie held strong, compelling, and often angrily expressed opinions on immigration (against), capital punishment (in favour) and homelessness (druggies and lazy bastards). These views were formed after considerable research on the echo chamber of his social media accounts. But not being able to see the remote control from where he was sitting, Jamie left the TV running. Yawning, his attention was unexpectedly drawn to the TV screen by the appearance of Sam's photograph. Having only caught the end of this item, a request for information and a phone number, he had no idea why she'd been featured. She hadn't come crawling back to him as he'd expected, but she would. He was convinced Sam could not stay away for long; she would be frightened of the consequences.

His vague thoughts about this were interrupted as Michelle sidled into the room.

"What's up with you?" he said. "You look like you've put on a few more pounds. Aren't you following that diet I gave you?"

"We're going to need some help tonight. Two of the waiting staff have called in sick."

"Can't you even deal with that?" Jamie rolled his eyes and sighed. "For fuck's sake, get some cover in."

"We're not that busy, so I thought you might help out."

"Listen. I'm the brains here, you're the fucking plodder. Get it sorted."

"I just thought…"

"Don't fucking think. You don't have the equipment."

"Why do you constantly…?"

"Oh, it's just a joke, for fuck's sake. Get a sense of humour." Locating the remote control, Jamie flicked through the channels. "By the way," concentrating on the TV screen, he didn't bother to look at her, "did you see the news just now? That woman, Sam, who worked here, her photo was on."

"No. Sorry." Anxiously, Michelle looked at him. "I didn't see it. I was too busy."

"She wasn't looking her best."

"Well, you'd be the expert on that."

Shrugging, Jamie went into the bedroom to change. Michelle was becoming clingy and he wanted rid of her. On a whim, he emailed the businessman with whom he had dealt so lucratively over the woman Sam.

II

Sarah Pritchard blinked nervously in front of a bank of cameras and lines of reporters. She was unwavering in her commitment to get through this for Robert, however much of an ordeal it became. He had believed in the absolute importance of truth, the value of duty, and the full accountability of those in power. These were his ideals, he had spoken of them many times both in private and in public, and Sarah had no intention of letting him down.

To the left sat her solicitor, Becky Scott, with the Assistant Chief Constable, Steven Doyle, on her right. The conference room was as stark as an underground bunker, and the sound of chairs scraping across the hard floor became a constant distraction. More reporters than expected had arrived; all the chairs had been taken and the others stood around the sides. Steven Doyle had never seen this level of interest before; the national press and broadcasters were all here, although no cameras were allowed in the room itself, by order of the security services. Doyle had no idea why that was important.

Watching and listening as he waited for everyone to settle down, Doyle was still fuming about the decision taken somewhere up the line, that they should immediately 'go public', in view of the deceased's status within government. In public, they were seeking witnesses, anxious that every part of this investigation appeared transparent and convincing, with no hint of anything being missed. Or covered up. In private, a decision of suicide had already been decided upon, reached without proper investigation. Word had been passed down, under the umbrella of 'national security', the inquest was to be held behind closed doors.

Initial forensic results showed loss of blood from a knife wound to his right wrist and an empty container of Co-Proxamol. To Doyle this was a farce; it was far too early for such results to be made public, no post-mortem had yet been carried out.

Immediately he heard his orders, obviously nothing was traceable or in writing, Doyle had tried to contact the chief constable, only to be told his superior officer was likely to be unavailable for several days. This was no surprise, the chief constable being notorious for 'encouraging the development of other officers through delegation', whenever a sensitive case appeared on his desk.

Sarah and Robert Pritchard had met in their final year at university. He was studying chemistry, she was reading English. On the face of it they had nothing in common, he came from a background of privilege, her family lived on a social housing estate in Nottingham. But Robert was charming and kind and avoided other independently educated students in favour of spending time with Sarah and her friends. Gradually their shared interests overcame their outward differences and they became lovers. She introduced him to theatre, he spoke excitedly about DNA and how he wanted to help cure cancer. To his friends she was his 'bit of rough'. Her friends worried he was just using her to help pass the time before he returned to Marlow and his parent's house by the river. To each other, they were partners. Inseparable and exclusive. Now, nearly twenty years and two children later, Sarah felt lost. Police questions about his work mystified her, enquiries about the state of their marriage infuriated her. Their son Robin, who was about to start university, was not coping at all well and hadn't spoken since hearing the news. He had worshipped his father. Their daughter Emily, studying for A-Levels, tried to help Sarah through each day, but her mother heard the crying every night from her bedroom. It was just seventy-two hours since their world was ripped apart.

Prior to the media conference, Doyle had sat in his office and considered every option. Photographs around the walls showed him in full uniform, proudly accepting awards for bravery, for saving lives, for leading the team who brought a serial killer to justice. And now he was tasked with providing a smokescreen to cover up a reckless disregard for rules of evidence, stamping on his belief in justice and service to the community. How could he square that circle? Clenching his jaw, he silently cursed the chief constable, using every slanderous and obscene word he could summon up from twenty-five years of dealing with killers, rapists, paedophiles, and the rest of society's dregs. It didn't make him feel any better. His commanding officer was keeping his head down, probably because he was fully aware this was a conspiracy. Taking a deep breath and checking his watch, Doyle stood and straightened his uniform, before heading down to the conference room.

Sarah Pritchard spoke falteringly about her husband, his belief in science as a force for good, his dedication to the work, and the devotion he had for their children. Twice Doyle passed her a glass of water, sensing she was becoming overwhelmed.

"We are looking for anyone in the area at the time. Anyone who might have witnessed what happened." Doyle took over as Sarah began to struggle. Against his better judgement they had agreed to take questions.

"Was this a walk your husband regularly made?" A female journalist Doyle didn't recognise spoke first.

"Not regularly." Sarah spoke softly, but firmly. Doyle noticed she was looking up above the heads of those in front of her. "But it was one of the walks he most enjoyed." Pausing briefly, she took a deep breath. "It was a walk he would take when he wanted time alone to think."

"Then you think there was something specific on his mind?"

"I…I don't know." She looked at Doyle, then towards Becky. "Maybe…"

"What distance would it be?" A different questioner, his voice dominating other attempts at being heard. "Approximately."

Becky leaned across, put her hand over the microphone, and spoke into Sarah's ear.

"I don't know. Three miles, maybe." Sarah Pritchard looked at her hands, slowly turning her wedding ring around her finger.

"Did you ever walk with him on that route?" A different male voice, it sounded younger, but Doyle couldn't tell who had spoken.

"I don't think that's relevant." Doyle stepped in before Sarah answered.

"No." Sarah's answer was barely audible. "I never did."

"How long…" A female voice started to ask a question, but Sarah raised her voice to interrupt.

"Someone must've seen him." She spoke quickly, leaning forward, half out of her seat. "Please. There must have been someone else there. Or near there. On his walk. Please." Her voice faltered and she slumped back into the chair.

"My client needs a few minutes." Becky Scott leaned across and put her hand over the microphone. In full agreement, Doyle reached over and switched it off.

They left the room.

"Please keep your seats." A plain clothes officer spoke from the podium. "They'll be back shortly." Having spoken, he followed the others.

After about twenty minutes they all returned. Doyle glared around as he steered a bewildered-looking Sarah back into her seat. Becky was talking quietly but urgently to Sarah as they both resumed their seats.

"We'll take some more questions." Doyle spoke bluntly, deciding against thanking those present for their patience.

"I understand there were no traces of blood where the body was found?" Doyle recognised Louise Ruck, a scrupulous and very methodical reporter from the local newspaper. "Can you confirm that?

"No."

"I spoke to the helicopter pilot who was searching for Dr Pritchard and he couldn't understand why his heat-seeking equipment hadn't registered anything."

"Both those statements are pure conjecture, and both are matters for the inquest."

"Mrs Pritchard, do you believe your husband was under so much pressure that he took his own life?" A male voice, from the national media, Doyle supposed.

"There was nothing to suggest... I mean, I didn't notice... our home life was separate from his work." Looking down at her hands clasped together on the desk, Sarah squeezed them harder, as though wanting it to hurt. "We wanted it that way... he wanted it that way... he was a good man... I don't understand these questions." Raising her voice, Sarah's face began to crumple, and tears began to form. "That evening... he was just...normal... just that... nothing else."

"No more questions." Doyle stood and began to guide Sarah Pritchard through the double doors adjacent to the platform. Turning around to face the room, she visibly took a deep breath and stared directly at the reporters.

"He wouldn't kill himself." She shrugged away Doyle's hand on her shoulder and spoke passionately. "Never. I knew him… it's unthinkable… he just wouldn't do that… you must understand." The strength and momentum of her words gradually faded. "Somebody must know… someone… please." Looking completely drained, she turned and left the room.

As he was about to follow the others out of the room, Doyle noticed a well-dressed man, with his back to him, deep in conversation with Louise Ruck. He was about six feet tall, Doyle judged, a full head taller than Louise, but she seemed to be doing most of the talking. Even from the distance of about six metres, Doyle could see her fierce expression, and noticed she regularly jabbed a forefinger towards the stranger.

In her early thirties, intelligent and resourceful, Louise was just about the only journalist Doyle trusted, an approval she had earned by being upfront and honest in all their dealings. During an horrific murder case two years ago, where a young female backpacker was strangled during a violent sex game, Louise had shared what she knew which led to an immediate arrest. In return, she gained some exclusive information which gained her some recognition from the national media. What also impressed Doyle was she avoided the lurid angle, ignoring the sex game angle jumped on by other newspapers, and focused on the truth. A young woman, Jessica Gordon was murdered, and her body dumped in the river with rocks strapped to it. The interview Louise carried out with her parents was thoughtful, avoided explicit or shocking details, and spared the distraught couple any further suffering.

Later, alone in his office, Doyle came to a decision. He needed to deal with this alone, sharing his plans with any of his officers could destroy their careers. He needed to start with Louise Ruck, not just because her information seemed to be better than his, and she would undoubtedly have a unique take on the case, but because his interest had been sparked by the conversation he'd observed.

III

In his office, Sir Anthony had been watching. Part way through he had begun pacing around, flinging out obscenities at the TV screen.

"What's that fool playing at?" Glowering towards Kristina, his angry look seemed to be blaming her. "Who gave permission for a press conference?" He slammed his open palm on the desk. "Why give that woman free rein? Witnesses? Jesus." Switching off the TV, he flung the remote control across the room, just missing Kristina's head. "That incompetent…" Rage seemed to prevent him from grabbing hold of a suitable adjective. "He was told, I assume?"

"Yes, but he probably felt…" Kristina's words were drowned out by Sir Anthony.

"Felt? I don't give a fuck what he felt. He had clear instructions, extremely clear, with no room for misunderstanding. I know that. I wrote them. I personally handed them to his chief constable." Barely taking a breath, Sir Anthony continued to vent his fury. "Allowing the woman to suggest there was somebody else involved. Can you not do one simple thing? I told you to get this sorted. I stressed it was vital. This is one big cock-up." He began to pace the room. "That man is a liability. I can't have him pissing around, putting our entire operation at risk." He leaned over Kristina, his face inches from hers. "I want him removed immediately and we'll take over the whole thing."

"If you don't mind me saying, Sir Anthony," as he moved away, she spoke slowly, choosing her words with care, "it will be difficult to take an investigation out of the police's hands without raising suspicions."

"So what? People get suspicious about all manner of things." He glared at her, but gradually regained some of his normal concentration, his voice

233

becoming lower as he sat down. "Conspiracy theories are ten-a-penny these days; social media petitions are raised for every pissing little gripe some moron gets a bee in his bonnet about. We can manage all that." Leaning forward, he pointed towards his assistant. "You need to focus on the job and not keep putting objections in the way."

"Sorry, Sir Anthony." Kristina chewed at her bottom lip and concentrated on keeping calm. "I was just trying to do my job. To point out possible pitfalls."

"Well, don't. You're not irreplaceable, you know."

"Sorry."

"And don't keep saying sorry."

Sensing Sir Anthony was looking for another subject to rant about, Kristina kept quiet, but her eyes blazed. This was a position she had worked hard to get, a career her parents could not stop talking about, proud of her regular promotions. They had both worked two jobs to afford the private one-to-one tuition that helped Kristina achieve exceptionally high grades and a first in history from Warwick University. She wasn't going to let them down, whatever she had to put up with. For the last seven years, Kristina had been recognised by her employers as a dedicated and meticulous member of staff, yet this man spoke to her as if she were a piece of shit on his shoe, just like her father had described being treated when he first came to the UK.

"So, I'll give you a name for the inquest." Turning to face her, he smiled as if his previous words had never been spoken. "A safe pair of hands. We'll delay it for as long as is possible, let all the curiosity die down. You can manage to organise that, I suppose."

"Yes."

"Good. Suicide will be the verdict. All documents to be kept out of the public domain for seventy years."

"Understood."

"This fellow Moss has been appointed?" Recognising the signs, Kristina understood Sir Anthony had no further interest in the death of Dr Pritchard and expected no further problems. He had made his point and moved on. She was now to ensure his wishes were carried out and prevent him having any further need to become involved. In the three years she had been working for him, Kristina had become familiar with this pattern. It suited her, and the occasional rollicking was an acceptable, if unpleasant, downside, in return for the autonomy it brought her.

"He has." Kristina smiled. "It was confirmed this morning."

"Good. Set up a meeting with him. I want to make him fully aware of the importance of our project. Especially the crucial second phase." His phone rang and, checking the caller ID he didn't answer until she had left the room.

Kristina left him sitting at his desk. Outside his office, she realised she'd forgotten her document case. Turning, she was about to knock when she heard him shouting.

"I want him dealt with. Understand. Yes. Whatever you think. Same arrangement."

Lowering her arm, she decided to return later.

IV

In the park, without giving any appearance of doing so, Claire watched the American as he strolled towards her. Well over six feet tall, with everything about him on the same scale, Jack Coburn paused frequently, taking in the activity around the lake. Spring was performing its annual miracle, daffodils standing proud, bushes in bud and moorhens sitting on their nests. In a few short days ducks and swans would be leading their young through the water.

"Claire." Sitting at the other end of the bench, Coburn continued to look towards the lake. A grey suit matched his close-cut hair, the regulation tie was deep blue with a logo Claire didn't recognise. Anyone watching would see a businessman taking a break, relaxing on a park bench, and enjoying the spring sunshine.

"Jack."

"This is a pleasant surprise." His accent was soft, mid-western, his smile devastating. "It's been a while." Joggers, both young women with earplugs, clearly very fit, ran past them. Neither Claire nor Jack spoke again until they had jogged well out of earshot, and Coburn waited before handing Claire one of the two take-away coffees he'd brought with him. "Are we here to celebrate this beautiful spring morning, or is there something I can do for you?"

"Sorry, Jack. It's business." Sipping her coffee, Claire waited until a woman with a pushchair had passed. She was young, manoeuvring the expensive-looking pushchair with one hand, leaving the other free for the phone she was talking into. A nanny, Claire guessed; very few parents took their kids for walks around the area, they were far too busy in high pressure jobs. Once more, her decision not to have children crossed her mind, and once more she recognised it was the right decision. How much older did she need to get before it simply stopped being an issue. "Forgive me for being blunt, Jack." Claire spoke quietly, still looking towards the lake. "Do you have any agents passing information from my department?"

"Now," he replied, "that's a strange question."

"And?"

"We don't." He paused. "But someone does."

"Who?" Claire took a sharp breath.

"I'm really not sure. But you need to be careful." He sipped his coffee. "The word is you've got something going, that some player wants in on. A big player."

"We are talking at government level?"

"I would guess so."

"Can you look into it for me? See what you can find out?"

"I'll check it out." Standing, he swallowed the rest of his coffee and dropped the container in a bin. "The next meal is on you."

"Absolutely." Waiting until he disappeared from her sight, she stood and slowly made her way back to the office. So deep in thought was she, a cyclist had to swerve to avoid her, giving her a volley of abuse. An idea began to form in her mind.

V

Hacking met Rader met in a local pub, The Brewer. Live music was playing; a band called The Singing Detectives was making enough noise to prevent their conversation being overheard. The tracker on Quinn's car had revealed nothing of any interest. He had been driving around randomly, as far as Hacking could make out, but only ending up at his apartment, where he presumably found the body. Almost two hours later, the car had been driven to another location, a house owned by Abi Collier, where it remained overnight.

"The woman?" Irritated by having to spend another evening in Rader's company, Hacking hoped to cut short this meeting. He hated complications, but he was being very well paid for this job.

"Sorted."

"Good." Mentally ticking off another assignment, he turned an appraising stare towards the thin man opposite. "Any problems?"

"Nah." He grinned. "Sweet as." Rader's smirk irritated Hacking.

"Did she tell you anything?" Raising his eyebrows, Hacking made no move towards looking away from the other man's eyes. "I take it you asked?"

"Yeah. Course." Rader lifted his pint glass, bringing his hairy-backed hands into the other man's view. As always, this sight repulsed Hacking and he looked away, knowing that image would leave him nauseous all day. Perfect hands for a gorilla, he often thought, Rader's true character portrayed physically. "She didn't know nothing."

"I see." Sipping his mineral water, Hacking curbed his usual impulse to condemn Rader's beer drinking. Another lecture on the health benefits of real ale was not what he needed right now. "You wouldn't by any chance be leaving out some details?"

"Nah. Course not."

"Did you find her address?"

"Nothing on her."

Hacking noticed Rader's sneer and watched him calmly gazing around the pub. He had no doubt the thug was lying.

"That's certainly unfortunate."

"Yeah." Rader shrugged. "Goes like that sometimes."

"So, that's it, is it?" Anger flashed across Hacking's eyes, and his voice grew harsher, like a developing storm, as he stared into the eyes of the man opposite. "It goes like that sometimes?"

"Yeah. It's a bummer."

Before he could answer, Hacking's phone rang. Checking the number, and with one final death stare at Rader, he stood and walked into the empty beer garden, hoping for better news about the other side of this job, his insurance policy, in case of any difficulties arising with the first option. Hacking liked to be thorough. Always have a back-up was a lesson he learned the hard way at the beginning of his career. In those early days he needed to learn quickly.

The teacher was his Uncle Jeff, his mother's brother, a businessman, smartly dressed, always carrying wads of cash, and driving the most upmarket cars.

"Why don't you come in with me. Old son?" Hacking remembered Jeff saying through a cloud of cigar smoke, on one of his rare visits "I could do

243

with a good right-hand man." The slap around Hacking's back that accompanied this statement almost knocked him off his feet.

"You stay away from Jeff," both his parents warned. "He's got his finger in too many pies."

"Heading for a fall," said his mother.

"And he's a fraud," added his father. But they both roared with laughter at his stories.

His money's real enough, Hacking remembered thinking.

"You want in?" Jeff said.

"Yes." Hacking saw pound signs.

"OK. You're on the payroll."

Hacking's first impression was that Jeff seemed to be out to lunch all day, yet the business poured in. All of it borderline legal; cars that had been written off, payday loans at extortionate rates, providing labour for new building developments, were the closest to legitimate activity. Jeff was the go-to man in that area for any 'under the table' transaction, and he was raking in the cash. Hacking saw suitcases full of cash being delivered; part of his role in the early days was to count it and keep a private record of monies owed and paid. Over time, having discovered Hacking's flair for strategy, Jeff expanded his involvement in the business.

When a client became difficult, or tried to avoid paying, Hacking was given the responsibility of devising and organising what Jeff termed 'the chastisement'.

He loved setting it all out, plotting a way through to the required result. Especially, he enjoyed watching each piece of the plan falling into place. Delighted by Hacking's skills, Jeff began to include him in the firm's highly profitable illicit activities. Blackmail and killing were the most lucrative.

"We need to get you some offshore bank accounts, old son."

Within eighteen months Hacking realised his ideas and plans were generating huge sums of money, amounts that weren't reflected in his income.

"It's my business. I take the risks. So, I earn a 'risk premium'." Jeff's explanation did nothing to overcome Hacking's irritation.

In this world, he learned, weakness will be exploited without a second thought. He set himself the task of taking over. Jeff needed to be punished for his greed. But punishment with impunity was the key, otherwise it would be for nothing.

It took a further nine months before Hacking was ready. In January 1990, Jeff's body was found washed up on the riverbank. Cause of death was a single bullet through the back of his skull. It was the first contract Hacking issued, and no one had ever been charged with the murder. Hacking reassured the clients, proved his worth with a much expanded and diversified selection of services. Thirty years later, he still worked with impunity, helped by the anonymity of the dark web and friends in high places. He had also created The Divine Path, an evangelical Christian organisation through which money could be laundered and moved offshore. By this time, he had five different identities, all with passports and separate bank accounts.

In the beer garden, well away from any eavesdroppers, Hacking answered the phone.

"Moss has been confirmed in position." It was a male voice, nasal and almost lifeless.

"Excellent." He moved further away from the building. "And you've checked him out?"

"As you requested."

"Anything I should know about?"

"Married, one daughter at uni." There was a pause, Hacking waited. "He likes a flutter."

"Really? Horses? Football?"

"Pretty much anything, by the look of it." The listless voice continued as if reading a list of destinations through a railway station loudspeaker. "Not huge amounts, but regular."

"Does he have any debts?" Hacking's mind began working, already piecing together an approach if it became necessary.

"Some. Small stuff. A couple of bookies. Payday loans. Five grand tops."

"That's extremely useful." Still checking around, Hacking walked into the car park.

"He's had gambling debts before, a couple of years ago. He owed money to The Wolfman. There were threats made." Another pause. "His old man bailed him out but wasn't too happy about it."

"So, a small amount of pressure is all it would take?"

"Yeah. Easy." The nasal voice livened up slightly. "He'll fold at the first hurdle."

"Get me a breakdown of his debts, could you? Exact amounts, who holds them. Chapter and verse."

"No problem."

The line went dead. A thin smile spread slowly across Hacking's lips as he made his way back into the pub. Returning to their table, he stood for a moment watching Rader who was still sitting there, an empty glass in front of him, his attention fixed on a group of three young women at the table diagonally opposite.

"Get us another, will you. I'm getting thirsty." Rader's eyes stayed on the women.

"You know, booze is like sex. Exciting to begin with, then just a habit."

"Well, they both work for me." Handing his glass to Hacking, Rader gave a low guttural sound. "You should try one of them. A bit of sin would do you good. Loosen you up a bit."

"Please keep your advice to those who wish to hear it. I do not."

Carrying Rader's beer and his own mineral water back, Hacking paused at the sight of an empty table.

Frowning, he checked around and soon discovered Rader talking to the young women, one of his hands resting on the nearest woman's shoulder. Shuddering at the thought of those hairy-backed hands, Hacking sat down to wait, expecting some sort of scene, certain they wouldn't put up with Rader for long. He was right. Almost immediately, one of the women stood, hands on her hips, and glaring at him.

"Will you go away?" In her late twenties, Hacking guessed, with an educated voice that was also extremely loud. Her glare alone would terrify anyone with an ounce of sensitivity, but Rader took no notice. Murmurs of approval flowed from the woman's two companions. "We don't want a drink, we certainly don't want to go on somewhere, and my friend wants you to take your disgusting hands off her."

The confrontation, Hacking noticed, had attracted significant interest from the other customers, most of whom were now looking in their direction, but Rader made no attempt to move. The woman started jabbing her finger towards him. "You're not funny, your disgusting innuendo is primary school stuff, and you look and probably smell like a tramp." Silence set in throughout the bar, as she sat down. Belatedly, a young member of staff sauntered over, asking if they needed any help.

"The day I need any help from any man, let alone a runt like you, will be the day I stop eating and drinking."

Rader sat back down opposite Hacking.

"So, you've successfully drawn attention to us. Feel better?"

"Just banter." Rader grinned. "You can't win a lottery if you don't buy a ticket."

"Well, now's not the time or place."

"Lighten up. What's your problem with the skirts?"

"You need to concentrate." Hacking grabbed Rader's wrist, preventing the beer getting to his mouth. "This isn't some game."

"I'm on a promise anyway. The woman next door's been coming on to me for weeks."

"Look. You're being very well paid." Hacking struggled to keep his voice level.

"Yeah, yeah. Fucking relax a bit, will you?" Rader paused, jerking his head towards the band. "See the guitarist?"

"I do."

"That's Quinn. I owe him one."

"Listen to me." Failing to hide his irritation, Hacking regretted the physical contact with Rader and backed away from grabbing any part of him for a second time. "A time and a place. No distractions. Not now."

"I'm off for a smoke." Without waiting for an answer, Rader headed out into the beer garden. He was growing tired of Hacking's orders, his weird righteousness, and the constant demand for answers. Rader had no intention of doing this for the rest of his life; his destiny wasn't to be small time; this was not going to get him the things he wanted. He was here to be something special. Drawing deeply on his cigarette, Rader decided to get out after this job. His skills would be in demand, violence would always be in demand, all he needed was to put the word out. He'd been approached about a month ago by from a drug gang looking for an enforcer, that would be perfect. Having graduated from elementary mugging and house-breaking, Rader had no intention of returning to either. His expertise lay in sadism; having discovered that, he'd never looked back. He would deal with Quinn first.

While Rader was outside, the women he had been trying to entertain prepared to leave. The loud one paused in front of Hacking.

"A friend of yours, is he?"

"No." Shrugging, Hacking pointed to the door. "He's gone for a smoke. If you want to avoid him, use the other exit; if you want to kick seven bells out of him, be my guest."

"I wouldn't lower myself." With that they all left the pub, passing and ignoring the returning Rader.

"Listen to me." Lowering his voice, Hacking smacked the palm of his hand on the table. "This is not some two-bit trick, it's big. The biggest dance in town. A one-hit to set us up for life." He lowered his voice until it was almost a whisper, but his eyes sliced through the other man. "So, don't you mess it up." His stare didn't waver. "Understand this, if you do, I'll personally slice you up and feed you to the pigs."

"OK, OK. Don't get out of your pram." Rader turned his head to one side. "Jesus, man. I've busted my guts on this, done a bang-up job. Show a bit of respect, yeah?"

"Respect?" Somehow, Hacking's stare increased in intensity, as if he were moving from conventional weapons and going nuclear. "You're small time, Rader, cheap. You've got no connections, no brains. Without me you would be worth zero. Remember that." He leaned back, still simmering but satisfied with Rader's silence, before putting an envelope in front of him. "The balance in cash for the last job."

"Cheers."

"Although I've had some strange conversations about your dealing with Dr Pritchard."

"Yeah, well. People gossip."

"They do." Hacking was anxious to get away. "Now, crawl back to whatever hovel you call home." As soon as Rader left, he took out a packet of antiseptic wipes for both hands and his face.

As he drove home, Hacking considered the end game with Rader. After this last job, he would be dispensed with. Thugs like him were ten-a-penny, so a replacement would be easy to find. The back-up plan for Moss involved subtlety and charm, neither of which Rader would recognise even if they came with labels and full instructions. Rader was also becoming increasingly distracted by a growing obsession with Quinn and was certainly going to become a liability, maybe even a threat to Hacking's own security. No spiritual guidance would be needed over Rader's fate.

VI

Arriving home, Hacking immediately took a shower. Spending any time with Rader always left him feeling soiled and worried about catching some unmentionable disease. The shower not only washed away any physical germs, it also improved his mood. Generally, he enjoyed two showers each day, more if he had spent time with other people. He paid for a cleaner (on minimum wage) to wash his clothes and to scrub down every surface each day, a hairdresser came every four weeks, and the house was deep cleaned quarterly. One personal assistant arrived every morning to ensure everything ran smoothly. For the more personal services, once a week he indulged himself in the carnal pleasures provided by a nearby agency; he had extremely specific desires, and the young lady joined him in prayer both before and after his gratification.

His property was set in two acres of land, in a remote village, with high walls surrounding the whole plot. Entrance to the grounds was restricted to one set of electric gates, with cameras recording all movement. Similar security defended his house, with several alarms and cameras covering all parts. Other than a minefield, Hacking had every available device designed to protect property, and he would have had the minefield, if he could find a trader to set it up. A gardener arrived daily, to keep the grounds under control; although Hacking had never met him, he approved of the results.

He enjoyed living in the remote village; there was a convenience store, a pub, and a church, but nothing much else. Not that he had ever availed himself of their services. Nobody bothered him. Almost every property there was similarly protected, he noticed, while driving in and out.

In his password protected ground floor office, his desk surrounded by security screens, Hacking considered the next move. Opening his business email account, he was delighted by the sight of one new enquiry for his services. No specific details at this early stage, as was normal, but it came from a high profile and very wealthy businessman. Hacking replied in general terms, suggesting a meeting.

Hacking was well-known to be meticulous in his planning, painstaking in preparation for every possibility, and clear-sighted about the client's required result. Such skills were the basis of his reputation, and the high esteem in which he was held by powerful people with problems. Or desires. Prayer was a great help, of that he was certain; it was a support system that assisted him in everything he achieved. Hacking prayed every morning and evening in an upstairs room set aside for that purpose, feeling eternally indebted to its power. It was his rock, a pillar keeping him strong in the face of temptation, and sustaining his commitment to accomplishing God's will. He attended most monthly meetings of The Divine Path, gratified by the regular increase in attendees. On occasion he spoke to the gathering, but often just watched from his personal vantage point overlooking the ground floor.

Sitting at his desk, he continued to work on his back-up plan for his own mission, having chosen the ideal individual to carry it through. If needed, Dr Moss would soon discover how quickly his ordered life would fall apart, the sleepless nights with no end in sight he would endure, and how completely he would belong to Hacking. None of this may be necessary, but he would be ready.

One other matter was still preying on his mind. There were conflicting stories about Pritchard's killer.

Day Five

Chapter 10

I

After completing their follow-up interviews, checking details, covering much the same ground as before, the police left Abi's house with the warning that neither Quinn nor Abi should leave the area without informing them.

"That's just cop-speak for 'we can't think of anything else to say'." Offering this explanation through habit, as nothing in Abi's expression suggested that she needed reassuring, Quinn began to doubt his wisdom in keeping the note secret. Too late now, he shrugged.

"Yeah, I've heard it before." Looking more relaxed than Quinn felt, Abi sat down and fussed over both dogs.

They lapsed into silence, a mood which transmitted itself to Buster and Hero, who sat quietly on the floor, staring at Abi. Quinn got the impression they were both blaming him for Abi's lack of attention.

Quinn lay back in his seat and stared at the ceiling, his mind sifting through the facts so far, and at a loss to know how to proceed. How could he get the contents of each phial analysed? There was no one he could think of who had any skills in that area. And what of Adam? He was no closer to tracing him; indeed, the likelihood of that ever happening seemed to be drifting further away.

Hearing Abi moving, he lowered his gaze and watched her leave the room.

"Don't ask me," he said to the dogs, shrugging. "Your guess is as good as mine." They both regarded him with open contempt.

Deciding to update the Controller, mostly in the hope she would help point to a way forward, he frowned as the phone went unanswered. Cancelling the call, Quinn chewed at his lower lip, his breathing becoming quicker. There might be nothing for him to worry about, but this hadn't happened before.

"We need to go." Abi returned with a backpack. Both dogs jumped up, tails wagging.

"What? Where?"

"I'll tell you on the way."

"Abi." Sitting down, Quinn's brow creased. "It doesn't work like that. I need to know before we start."

"Why?"

"We've had this conversation before. This won't end with you being fined or bound over, or whatever. Look what they did to Sam."

"Thanks for reminding me, Ace. Yeah. OK. I get it." She stroked Buster for a few seconds. "We need to bring the dogs."

"You're not listening to me."

"You really are a detective," she said. "Anyway, I've been thinking about Adam."

"Funnily enough, so have I."

"There are no cops outside." She smiled and stretched her back. "We can go."

"We could, but to where?"

"We'll need your car this time. And a change of clothes. It'll be an overnight trip." Moving towards the door, she half-turned. "You can buy me something to eat on the way."

"Tell me where we're going."

"Not yet." Staring directly at Quinn, a look that cut right through him, Abi obviously wanted there to be no misunderstanding. "I'm not sure I can trust you."

"You don't have much choice."

"Oh, but I do. I know where Adam will be. You don't." A small smile of triumph played at her mouth for a few seconds. "Shall we go?"

II

Hacking had prepared his Plan B for Dr Moss and one telephone call had sealed the deal. Simon Freeman's skills as a conman were venerated by those in the know and Hacking had employed him twice in the past, so making use of his talents in this matter was an easy decision to make. They had spoken by phone and Simon was putting together a strategy, based around horse racing, that would leave Moss at the mercy of Hacking. A meeting was agreed for the following day.

Before then, Hacking needed to make some enquiries about the death of Dr Pritchard. Although it wasn't a major issue - the outcome had been exactly as required - the conflicting stories were playing on Hacking's mind. He disliked loose ends and needed to know the truth. Rader had given his version, so he decided to call upon a contact in the security service; they would surely know the truth as Pritchard had worked for them. Hacking's contact was someone who owed him, who would now be in prison were it not for Hacking's personal intervention and problem-solving skills. Since that moment, four years earlier, that client had become a member of The Divine Path and a valuable contact, whose connections had twice smoothed the way to success for Hacking's projects. He was also Hacking's source of information concerning the research aims but was unaware that The Divine Path creator's view ran counter to his own. It was a situation Hacking had no intention of remedying; every source of intelligence had a value and this contact's usefulness had not yet expired.

They spoke at length and after ending the call, Hacking understood two things. Firstly, Pritchard had been warned to concentrate on the science and to stop meddling in matters of policy. Secondly, by disregarding these instructions, he had been considered a wild card and an active threat to the nation. His death had, therefore, been demanded at the highest level and was carried out by one of their own agents. His contact had no doubts about that.

Day Five

Chapter 11

I

Adam scrambled through a window at the back of the hotel, ran across the main road, past the Co-op supermarket and on to the station forecourt, where he jumped into the lead taxi. He shouted to the driver to head for Robin Hood's Bay, the agreed meeting place, where Abi may be waiting. It was a long shot; even as he spoke the words, Adam knew that. But he had nowhere else to go. This was his last roll of the dice.

Charged forty-five pounds for a twenty-minute drive, Adam thrust a fifty-pound note into the driver's hand, jumped out of the cab, and told him to keep the change. Later, he wondered if that was how they located him, his single spontaneous act of generosity, a mistake born out of urgency. At the time, he thought nothing of it.

It was too late to find accommodation, but the evening was warm, and Adam knew the area. Certain there would be a choice of empty boats, he headed down to the bay and eventually found exactly what he wanted, a small cabin cruiser, close to the shore, with a primitive lock on the cabin. Opening it easily and quickly, Adam found an ideal place to spend the night. There were two bunks, several blankets, a hob, and a small TV. A toilet was through another door at the end of the cabin. A newspaper dated three weeks earlier lay on the small table, which Adam took to indicate the boat was not in regular use. In a cupboard he found a ring binder and replaced the contents with his own notes. Avoiding lights and anything else that could give away his presence to anyone passing by, Adam settled down and continued reading through his notes.

Notes:

Dr Pritchard is dead. I saw the headlines in the newsagents. They say it was suicide - I don't believe that, and I never will. He was so determined to reveal the truth, so positive and strong, and resolved to using his knowledge and understanding to bring down this attempt at tyranny. So, he must have been murdered. There is no other explanation. He was killed because they were afraid of what he knew, of how he could destroy their brave new world, the taking over of state power by corporate interests. Please, whoever you are, tell people Dr Pritchard did not kill himself. It's all on this memory stick, every piece of evidence, a stark and uncompromising exposure, shining a bright light into the places Power wishes to keep dark.

I believe the phase two initial vaccinations are fully prepared, and in a few weeks, maybe even days, they will have produced enough for their purpose. Power's long-term objective is simple, to create a society that will believe lies to be facts, that repetition means truth, that faith matters more than information. A society that celebrates Power's commitment to silencing opposition, to saluting the flag, and to promoting and nurturing prejudice against those who have different beliefs.

Firstly, Power's belief that people live in poverty only because they are stupid and lazy means this group will be targeted first; the poorest will be made sterile, as will their existing children. This will be the first action taken during phase two. Within twelve months, education and health care will be unavailable for those without the resources to pay for it, and the entire benefits system will be dismantled, therefore avoiding the situation where several generations of one family 'sponge' from the state. After all, food, housing, work, these are not 'rights', but have become dependencies through a state that panders to the weak and lazy. Harnessing the power of the state with that of the markets will save the country billions. Information held on the memory stick includes minutes of high-level meetings and fully- costed plans confirming this intention.

The group for whom I was one of the test dummies will continue to be engaged in creating divisions in society. Programmed for violence, their role will be to cut open the vein of people's grievances, stirring up disputes and anger on the streets and creating a mob mentality. It is so easy. Kill a white person in one area, a black person in another. Sit back and watch as the tension builds, then stir up the deceased's community. Switch over and provoke the other side and you have a riot. Burning mosques, temples, synagogues, any building not devoted to Christianity. This creates what they call 'The Fear' with the slogan 'Be loyal, Stay alert, Protect your culture', pushed at every opportunity. Huge posters by the roadside, on the sides of buses, in between TV programmes, and in every other space they can find. The fertility of these mercenaries will be increased, encouraging them to breed, ensuring violence becomes systemic. Their empathetic emotions will be destroyed - they will feel no pity, no sadness, no compassion. People over seventy, apart from the elite, will fall victim to heart attacks.

Then comes 'The Disappeared', Power's name for the rounding up of undesirables. External telecommunications will be jammed unless unequivocally approved by the government. This will all be part of the second phase and will happen very quickly. I don't know what will come after that, those plans were still being discussed.

Initially, all unskilled work will be carried out by low paid immigrants, allowed into the country for that purpose only, with their visas needing to be renewed annually. There will be no appeals process if that renewal is declined. Power anticipates that automation and AI will eventually remove any need for this group.

The proof is with Abi and on the memory stick. Our information is unassailable. Get this out there. Online would obviously get it out immediately, but it would last about three seconds before it was taken down. They will be watching everything. CEOs of media corporations will be in on this. But I have no choice. I need to find Abi, which is a risk for her that I never wanted to take. I have one chance. We had an agreed meeting place, if ever we were being investigated. We have never used it and she will probably want nothing to do with me, but it's worth a try.

II

Arriving at the small independent coffee shop in response to Doyle's telephone call, Louise moved across to the corner table where he was sitting. Café by the Arch, so named because it sat next to the remains of one Roman entrance into the town, was a tiny place, with three tables inside and two on the pavement, usually full and busy with a queue of takeaway orders.   Today, surprisingly, Doyle was the only customer.

"Your presence here doesn't seem to be good for business." Louise grinned. "Or have you commandeered the place?"

"Louise, thank you for agreeing to meet me." Smiling as he stood, Doyle shook her hand, before indicating she should sit down.

"I prefer Lou." When she smiled, her entire face lit up. "Well, this is a surprise. Normally, it's the other way around, I'm always trying to get the police to talk to me."

"Yes, well, sometimes we need help."

"So I'm not in trouble then?" Teasingly, she spoke softly, her voice like a summer breeze. "No unpaid fines, no drunk and disorderly charges?"

"Not that I've been informed about."

Sitting in silence for a few moments, Doyle again questioned the wisdom of including Louise. Having thought long and hard about the pros and cons of involving the journalist, he again felt he had no choice. People who would never talk to the police would often speak to the press, and this was likely to be important.

"I can relax then."

"What were you and that man discussing after the press conference?" Looking at Louise, he saw a slight discomfort in her expression. "I hope you don't mind me asking."

"The usual shit." She made and held eye contact. "As I went to leave, he said, 'I bet it was one of your lot'. I asked him why he thought a journalist would kill a scientist; he just laughed. I asked him if he meant a black person."

"What did he say to that?"

"He said, and I'll remember the words forever. 'Of course. You're all still savages really'."

"You should've reported him." Shocked, Doyle had no idea what else to say. His own world view was divided between 'right' and 'wrong', nothing else.

"No point. He would just deny it." Forcing a tight-lipped smile and balling one of her hands into a fist, Louise maintained eye contact.

"I'm sorry you were subjected to that. Do you know who he was?"

"No." Leaning forward, Louise sipped her green tea. "Can we move on, please?"

"I'm going to level with you, Lou." Doyle's voice was quiet, but urgent. "The Dr Pritchard case, I'm not sure who I can trust, and I don't want to involve any of my officers." Pausing, he called for another coffee. "You were at the press conference, you asked interesting questions. I've seen your work. I'm going to take a leap of faith here and trust you."

"I don't know what to say."

"Yes or no will do."

"I get the story first?"

"You do."

"Then, yes."

III

Claire met Jack again in their usual place, this time at his request. Unusually, he was already waiting as she walked alongside the lake. This time she brought the coffee and handed him one before sitting down. There was a slight drizzle, but the bench was partly sheltered by a huge oak tree.

Further back and out of view, just behind a fountain, stood Kristina, wearing an earpiece.

"Jack. I wasn't expecting to see you again so soon."

"Claire. Just listen to me." Jack stared directly ahead, leaned forward, and lowered his voice, and Claire had to concentrate hard to catch every word. "What I'm hearing is some scary shit. I don't know what you people are doing over there and I don't want to. I'm swamped. But this is for real, Claire, and you need to watch your back."

"That sounds ominous." She took a sip of coffee and frowned. In the two years they had been intermittently sharing this bench, Claire had never known Jack to exaggerate.

"OK. Listen. I followed up as you asked, checked around, not too obviously. Did a bit of digging."

"Thanks, Jack."

"What I'm hearing is that some other agency, I don't know where, but I'm guessing Russia, China, maybe North Korea, want whatever it is you're doing." He continued to ignore his coffee. "What I'm hearing is that they have a contact at your end, keeping them in the loop. And whatever they're receiving is hitting all the right notes. They're wetting themselves."

Ignoring her coffee, Claire stared ahead, smiling grimly.

"You don't know what level their contact is?"

"Nope. Can't help you there. But I'm guessing it's pretty far up the ladder." Pausing, he glanced towards her. "I've got to lay off it for a while, I'm already getting the sideways looks."

It had to be the eugenics, but who could possibly be passing information? Quinn's question reappeared in her mind.

"Is the other matter sorted?"

"Sure is. And I hope it works."

"Thanks, Jack." Claire remained seated. "I owe you one."

"You sure do." Standing, and against all protocol, he turned to face her. "I'll keep an ear to the ground." Turning away, he stared towards the lake. "Watch yourself, Claire. I really want to be collecting on that debt."

"I will. Thanks, Jack." She checked her watch; it was almost time.

Deep in thought, she walked back towards her office. Once more she failed to notice something coming towards her. This time it was a car, travelling fast. When it hit her, she was catapulted into the air. Jack Coburn heard the thump and ran towards the incident. An ambulance arrived and Claire was carefully stretchered into the back. Coburn checked his watch and agreed to accompany the ambulance. If nothing else, he could identify the body.

Day six

Chapter 12

I

Jamie had given no further thought to seeing Sam's photograph on the TV, so he was surprised when the police arrived at the restaurant to talk to him. Having never been a morning person, and with the restaurant being busy the evening before, it took a while for Jamie to let them in.

"I hope we didn't get you up, sir." Detective Chief Inspector Barnard's smile suggested otherwise. "We'll sit here, shall we?" He pointed to a wooden table with plastic menus slotted into their wooden holder, alongside a solitary tulip sitting in a slender glass vase.

"Erm, yeah." Rubbing his eyes and trying to stifle a yawn, Jamie nodded. "That's cool." They were away from the window, two hours before the restaurant opened for lunch, so Jamie relaxed.

"Pizza Pete." Barnard glanced around, smiling. "Unusual name."

"It's easy to remember." Leaning back in his seat, Jamie smiled. "What can I do for you, gentlemen?"

"Do you recognise this woman, sir?" Placing a photograph in front of Jamie, Barnard didn't move his gaze from the man opposite. Initial reactions were always informative.

"I don't think so."

"Mmm. I see." Taking a fresh pack of mints from his pocket, Barnard slipped one into his mouth. "She used to work here, I believe."

"Samantha Watson," said George. "Preferred to be called Sam."

"Thank you, sergeant." Jamie was lying, Barnard saw the tell-tale expression on his face. "She was murdered not far from here."

"Oh… I don't… when?" Crossing his arms, Jamie looked up from the photo.

"In her diary for the day she was murdered, it states she was working here." Ignoring Jamie's question, Barnard began to crunch his mint. "Can you confirm that was the case?"

"I'd need to check."

"Of course, sir." After a few seconds, when Jamie hadn't moved, Barnard raised his eyebrows. "Now, if you don't mind."

"Oh, yeah. Sorry."

Standing, Jamie disappeared through a door marked 'Staff Only', from where some muffled conversation could be heard.

"Ever eaten in here, George?"

"More of a fish and chips man, myself, sir."

"Mm, well." Barnard looked around. "Fifteen tables. Take away as well. Watch your pizza being made. Nice little earner, I should think. What they call 'cool', I suppose."

"It always looks busy when I drive past."

"Grab one of those menus, George. We might as well take a look while we wait for Mr. Cousins to return."

"Sir."

"Not much of a smell is there? No food aromas." He sniffed the air. "Sort of fruity, I'd say."

"Yes, sir." Baker was used to his superior officer's apparently random thoughts. "I expect the cleaners have just finished."

"Yes, well." He ran a finger across the table and examined the result. "Mmm. Good point, sergeant. Keep thinking like that and we'll make a detective out of you yet."

"Sir."

"Where's he got to?" Frowning, Barnard stood and moved towards the 'Staff Only' doorway. "How long does it take to get a rota?" He looked back towards George.

"I suppose it depends, sir."

"Mmm. Depends on whether you've got anything to hide." At that moment, Jamie came back into the room. "Ah, I was getting worried about you, sir." Smiling, Barnard fixed his eyes on Jamie. "Thought you may have had an accident."

"Sorry. It's always a bit hectic at this time. My wife does the admin, but she's out."

"Well, never mind that." He held out his hand. "Let's have the rota then." He glanced at the date and passed the papers to his sergeant, while staring at Jamie. "Have a look through those, George. See what you can find."

"Sir."

"I notice, Mr. Cousins, that Sam Watson isn't listed as working that day."

"Sometimes shifts change at the last minute."

"Do they?" Pausing, he waited for any further information. "Do they indeed?"

"People going off sick." Jamie grinned. "At the last minute. It makes life difficult." He shrugged. "I'm sure you get it in your line of work, Inspector?"

"Yes, Well. We all have our crosses to bear, isn't that right, sergeant?"

"Certainly do, sir."

"You know she was killed that evening, sir? The twenty-third. She was abducted from The Adam and Eve pub about half a mile from here." Barnard leaned forward, moved the menu to one side, and clasped his hands together on the table. "Then tortured and murdered at a different location."

"I didn't know. Not always on top of the news, sorry." With his brow furrowed, Jamie gave his best shot at showing sorrow. "It's awful. Tragic."

"It's certainly that, sir." Calm and composed, Barnard turned his head to face the sergeant. "What do you think, George?"

"Murder is always dreadful, sir."

"Indeed." Staring at Jamie, noticing the lack of eye-contact, Barnard leaned back and spoke as if an idea had just occurred to him. "Did you know, Mr. Cousins, that most murders are carried out by a person known to the victim?"

"I think I've read that somewhere."

"Really? Mmm. Yes, well you can learn a lot from reading." Barnard's stare had once been described by George as capable of stripping wallpaper, and Jamie was squirming in his seat. "Your rota, for example. I expect we'll learn something from reading it, don't you, George?"

"I already have, sir."

"Really?" Without turning around Barnard's eyes widened, increasing the power he focused on Jamie. "That's excellent work, sergeant. Well done. Very quick. Don't you think, Mr. Cousins?"

"It's certainly quick."

"Share the good news, George. I think our friend here is impatient to know what you've discovered."

"A new waitress started the day after Sam disappeared."

"Really? Now that is interesting. Maybe, Mr. Cousins you knew someone would be unavailable from then?" Not waiting for an answer, he continued. "So, just how well did you know the deceased?"

"She worked for me." Shrugging, Jamie glanced away.

"So, you wouldn't be aware of any family or friends?" He paused to slip another mint into his mouth. "Or anyone who meant her any harm?"

"As I said, I didn't really know her that well."

"Make sure you get that down, sergeant." Barnard smiled. "He didn't know her very well." Raising his eyebrows, he turned to face his sergeant.

"We need to keep on top of everything. So we don't waste this gentleman's time. Anything else interesting in the rota?"

"Sam is listed as working the day before, but there's no mention after that. Not even an entry crossed out."

"Did you not wonder why she just disappeared?" Barnard's brow furrowed, as if he were trying to pin down a vague thought. "I would've thought she had wages owing, or a notice period to serve."

"It's a problem with this trade." Jamie shrugged. "People often leave without notice."

"Really?" Barnard turned to his sergeant again. "Were you aware of that, George?"

"No, sir."

"And do you owe her any wages?"

"I'll need to check."

"Of course. No need to do it now. Perhaps you could let us know."

Barnard placed his card in front of Jamie. "Details are all there." For a few seconds, Barnard held on to the other man's eyes. Then, he abruptly stood. "Anyway, come on George let's leave this gentleman to his business."

Jamie's boasting to friends about Sam and how he broke their relationship began to gnaw away at him. Would the police want to talk with them? How much would they remember? It wasn't long ago, but they were all drunk. And Michelle, what would she say? She knew about his relationship with Sam, he never took much trouble to hide his affairs.

"She pays me attention, which you don't," Jamie remembered saying when confronted by his wife. He couldn't remember what reply Michelle gave, but she was the key; the others could be explained by boasting, wanting to be admired, to be leader of the pack. Michelle was the weakest link. A response from the businessman quoted a high fee for 'taking care of Michelle'. He rang and they spoke for several minutes.

II

 The day crawled for Jamie, his mind on the police questioning, resulting in several complaints from diners about mistakes with their bills. When eventually the final customer left late that evening, Jamie selected the best red wine, collected two glasses, and indicated to Michelle that they should share it.

"I've been thinking." He spoke while pouring the wine. "About us."

"Really?" Nervously, Michelle stared at Jamie, her eyes wide. "What about us?"

"I realise you must feel neglected, Shell. I've been distracted. Working to pay the bills. Wanting to make this place successful for you." He paused and tried to make eye contact. "And you've been so distant, lately, I've been really worried about you." Jamie looked away. I didn't want to raise this, I thought we'd work it out. But you've given me no choice."

"I…"

"You spend too much time with your sister." He sounded upset. "She's never liked me. I know she tries to turn you against me. But you're so trusting, she takes advantage of you."

"Well…"

"No. It's fine." Jamie held up his hand. "Don't make excuses for her. We need to get these people out of our lives and stick together. You need to be strong. You're the most important person in my life and I just want to make you happy." He reached for her hand and squeezed. "You know that don't you?"

"I suppose…"

"But I don't always believe you feel the same."

"Were you sleeping with that waitress, the one who disappeared?" Looking directly at him, Michelle held her breath.

"Don't be ridiculous." Jamie believed if he could fake sincerity, everything else would be a doddle. "But you couldn't blame me if I did. You've always been too busy, too tired. Never making time for me."

"That's unfair." Michelle began to stand. "Anyway, I need time to figure out this stuff for myself. And I need to clear up."

"That's what I mean." Jamie held out both hands. "You always avoid me. Like I'm not important to you. What am I supposed to think?"

"I really don't know." Michelle sat back down. "I get confused sometimes."

"We need to stand together. Have each other's backs." Jamie reached out and Michelle took his hands. "Stop outsiders from creating doubts and creating rifts between us. Or their poison will destroy all that's great between us."

"I suppose…"

"So how about a trip to the West End, take in a show, a night in a hotel."

"What about the restaurant?"

"We can close for one night. Or get one of the staff to take charge."

"Well, Georgia is very capable."

"Then that's settled. Georgia it is." Home and dry, thought Jamie as he topped up their glasses. Back in the game. He could control this and forget about Sam. The businessman wouldn't be needed.

Day Six

Chapter 13

I

Abi programmed the sat-nav as Quinn drove. He didn't recognise the postcode, but realised they were heading for the Yorkshire coast. It was going to be a long drive. Buster and Hero were asleep on the back seat. Switching on the radio, Abi selected a music station, and sat back in her seat. Quinn sighed at what he considered to be over-produced and formulaic packaged sound, pressed his steering wheel controls, and knocked down the volume.

"That's cheating, Ace," she said, without moving her gaze from the side window.

"That's rubbish." He nodded towards the radio.

"Sorry, grandad." Then she was struck by a thought and turned to face him. "You didn't tell the filth we were going away?"

"Did you want me to?

"No way." She relaxed again. "The less they know, the better."

"Well, they'd have wanted to know where we were going and why." He accelerated on to the motorway. "And I have no idea."

"Yeah. Excellent."

"Then we're all good. You can tell me now."

"I suppose so." Abi screwed up her face a little, a habit Quinn had noticed whenever she needed to decide something important. It made her look about sixteen. "We had a meeting place." Staring at the road ahead, her voice softened, almost as though she was worried about being overheard. "In case either of us were threatened in any way." Quinn had dropped his speed a little to concentrate on what Abi was saying, but she paused to watch a truck overtake and then pull in close to them, forcing Quinn to drop back. "You know, if it was really serious, frightening."

"Sounds very sensible." Building up the speed again, Quinn kept his response neutral. Not asking questions, afraid of disturbing Abi's thoughts or making her clam up, Quinn let her continue at a pace she was comfortable with.

"We'd been protesting in Yorkshire, occupying a site of natural importance, and it got a bit hairy. Worse than normal. One day I got pinned to a wall by some bloke in a mask." Her voice dropped. "He really wanted to hurt me. You can always tell when it's serious."

"I can guess."

"He had me by the throat, so I jabbed my fingers hard into his eyes." Grinning at the memory, Abi turned her face towards Quinn. "He let go of me, so I kicked him in the bollocks. And I legged it out of there."

"Remind me not to get on the wrong side of you."

"We took a break, went to the coast." She spoke with a warmth he couldn't remember hearing before from her. "Stayed in a pub for a few nights."

"Sounds ideal."

"It was." He noticed a catch in her voice. "We just wandered around, doing nothing. Eating fish and chips, drinking beer. We even took a bus to Whitby and went up to Dracula's place. Spooky." Sighing, she looked towards Quinn again. "Sorry, Ace. You don't need to hear all this."

"It's better than listening to that sh… stuff." Nodding towards the radio, he grinned.

"We said if either of us were in trouble we would come back." A police siren sounded, making her jump.

"Nothing to do with us." He smiled at her reaction. "Why didn't you tell me this before?"

"We were to wait a week before meeting. That was yesterday. Then we would wait a further week. We didn't want to overreact. And it would give time for whoever caused the problem to lose interest."

"Seems sensible."

"There's another reason. I didn't want to lead you to him. It was our place. No one else was supposed to know." Her voice became fierce. "He'll feel betrayed."

"That's better than being dead." Hoping he sounded sincere, Quinn glanced at the sat-nav as it gave an instruction to take the second exit at the next roundabout. "And you did the right thing."

"Did I? For him, or for you?"

"For all three of us."

"Yeah. Right." Abi turned her face away and stared out of the window.

"That sat-nav voice is really irritating."

"Because its female?"

Glancing at Abi, Quinn wasn't sure if she was joking, so he took the safe option of saying nothing.

After driving for about ninety minutes, Quinn steered into a service station and parked as close as possible to the entrance.

"Something to eat?"

"Yeah." Abi had opened her door even before the engine cut off. "And a pee."

Walking quickly past a small amusement arcade, all flashing lights and jingle jangle sounds, and a mobile phone accessories shop, they reached the main forecourt.

"Cheeseburger and chips." Pointing to McDonalds, Abi smiled. "Large chips please. And a coffee. I'm off to the ladies."

"Well, yes, ma'am."

Finally, after queueing for what seemed an eternity, Quinn found Abi had already grabbed a table. Looking around at the crowded area, Quinn began to wonder where all these people were heading. Going away? Coming back? One large group were obviously on their way to a football match, mostly dressed in club shirts, all laughing and joking, and verbally abusing the day's opponents. For a split second, Quinn wished his trip were that straightforward. Winning and losing were completely different concepts in his world.

"Like football?" Swallowing a mouthful of burger, Abi looked from the supporters to Quinn.

"Not fanatically. I'll watch it on TV, not been to a live game for years. Rugby is my game."

"Sheffield United, me. The blades." Looking more relaxed than he had seen her before, Abi grinned. "So, union or league?"

"Union." Quinn paused as a woman dragging two young children barged into his shoulder as she pushed through. "That where you're from then?"

"Yeah. Just outside the city." Shovelling some chips into her mouth, Abi paused to chew. "You?"

"Milton Keynes. Roundabout city."

"Knew you were from the south." Immersed in their own thoughts, they finished eating in silence.

"Don't you have a driving licence?" Quinn asked as they returned to the car.

"No comment." Grinning, Abi climbed back into the passenger seat.

II

Following an early morning telephone call, or summons as it seemed to her, Sarah Pritchard sat in Kristina's small office, shocked by the younger woman's lack of compassion. There was no small talk, no attempt at expressing any sympathy about Robert's death. She had expected Kristina, at the very least, to acknowledge his loss to the scientific community, and politely ask how Robin and Emily were coping. Even if she didn't care. So many others had offered their condolences, he'd obviously been held in higher regard than even she realised. The constant flow of messages and cards had been a comfort, but Kristina's indifferent manner threw her off balance and it took Sarah a few moments to take in exactly what Kristina was saying.

"I'm sorry." She smiled apologetically. "Could you repeat that please? I'm finding it a little difficult to concentrate at present."

"So, Mrs Pritchard." Kristina sighed, which Sarah took as a sign of impatience. "As I was saying, your husband's death would normally allow you to claim his death-in-service benefit."

"That's what I've always understood, yes." Chewing at her lower lip, Sarah sensed a problem.

"It's a very large sum in your case."

"Well." Sarah struggled to keep her voice even. "He's worked for the government for a long time. Even when he could've earned more in the private sector." She didn't want to talk about money. She wanted Robert's contribution to the scientific community to be acknowledged.

"Well, in this case we do have a slight issue." Kristina ignored Sarah's comments and looked down at her notes. "Treason."

"I'm sorry?"

"Treason. Your husband betrayed his country. Is that easier for you to understand?"

"I know what treason means." Eyes blazing, Sarah gripped the arms of her chair. "I'm not stupid. What has it got to do with Robert?"

"I think we both know the answer to that." Kristina paused, then leaned towards Sarah. "However, we will honour the promised payment on one condition."

"Which is?" Sarah fought to hold back her anger. How dare this girl, not much older than Emily, treat Robert with such contempt.

"You will sign a confidentiality agreement, return any documents, both hard copies and those held on electronic devices of any kind. Our team will assist in this and are already on their way to your house. You are required to give them whatever assistance they demand, and to make no attempt to conceal anything relevant, or to destroy any document whatsoever, until the team have assessed it."

"I see."

"If you agree, and conform to these conditions, this is the amount you will receive." Sarah briefly glanced at the numbers pushed across the desk.

"That's a lot of money." She could think of nothing else to say.

"It is. You would be an extremely rich woman and able to give your children the best start in life. Robin and Emma, isn't it?"

"Emily. Not Emma."

"Ah, yes. Of course. Emily."

"It's money I'm entitled to." Disgusted by the lack of an apology for getting her daughter's name wrong, Sarah dug her fingernails into her palms.

"And your husband would want you to have it."

"I know better than you, how hard he worked. He gave his life to science in the service of this country." Tears rolled slowly down her cheeks.

A non-disclosure agreement was placed in front of Sarah and a pen offered for her signature.

"I'd like to read it." Her husband's advice when she had to sign anything came to mind. Smiling gently, Sarah remembered how he even read through website terms and conditions before ticking the 'I Agree' box.

"Of course. It's all legal speak, I'm afraid. National security issues. There's the usual clawback clause, of course, just in case you decide to renege on the agreement in the future."

Neither woman spoke again until Sarah had added her signature to the document.

"Thank you, Sarah." Another sheet of paper appeared. "And this is just to confirm our access to your home and our authority to remove any item that, in our opinion, may compromise national security."

"Do your worst. You won't find anything." Adding her signature to the second document, Sarah dried her eyes with a tissue.

"Because there isn't anything? Or because it's very well hidden?"

Sarah stared at Kristina but didn't reply.

Finding herself in the corridor, Sarah checked her watch and sent a text message, before making her way to the ground floor. Leaving the building, she stood on the pavement and waited. A response to her message arrived, followed a few moments later by a car. The passenger door was opened by the driver and Sarah climbed in, sinking back into the comfortable seat.

"Everything go OK?" Assistant chief constable Steven Doyle drove slowly away from the kerb.

"I think so."

"Good. I've set up the meeting we spoke about."

"They're on their way to search my house." Biting her lip, and seeming to hold her breath, Sarah dug around in her bag and pulled out her phone. "I need to phone Emily. Robin is away with friends."

"Of course." Doyle paused, uncertain how to phrase his next words. "Get her out of there. Has she friends she can go to?"

"Yes." Swallowing twice, all the colour drained from Sarah's face. "Is she in danger?"

"I don't think so, but it'll be upsetting, and she's already had a lot to deal with." Doyle took a deep breath and hoped he was right. "I'll turn off the Bluetooth, so you have some privacy."

III

Inspector Barnard arrived in the interview room carrying a file of papers, which he laid on the table. He nodded to Sergeant George Baker, then fixed his gaze on Jamie Cousins.

"For the recording, Detective Chief Inspector Barnard has entered the room." George spoke while still staring at Jamie.

"You've cautioned him, George?"

"I have."

"Good." Barnard pulled the only other chair up to the table and sat down, frowning as he flicked through the papers in front of him. Silence was a weapon with which Barnard was an expert, having made a career out of exploiting it. Timing was crucial. At the right moment, keeping quiet could create a vital opening, paving the way for anxiety, fear and even confession from any suspect. Watching Jamie closely, Barnard could almost smell the sweat pouring off him and could see the uncertainty in his eyes. This was the moment.

"Well, Mr. Cousins, it seems you've not been completely honest with us." Flicking through his papers he took out a single sheet, silently reading through the information for a few seconds. "So, is there anything you'd like to add to the statement you gave last time we spoke?"

"About what?"

"About what, he says, George."

"Sir."

"But he knows 'about what', doesn't he, George?"

"Of course he does, sir."

"Well, let's take your relationship with the deceased, for example." Scanning the sheet again, before staring at Jamie, he slowly shook his head. "When we first spoke, you described this relationship as one of employer and employee. Is that what you have written down in your notebook, George?"

"It is, sir."

"Well, there's my problem. This statement of yours isn't entirely true." Laying down the paper, he slipped a mint into his mouth. "Of course, there's a certain amount of truth there, as far as it goes. But it doesn't go far enough. It fails to convey the full extent of your relationship with Samantha Morton." Leaning forward, Barnard clasped his hands on the desk. "Now, why would you be trying to mislead me and my sergeant?"

"Well, I'm married." Jamie ran his tongue over lips that were almost stuck together. "Can I have some water?"

"I don't think we have water, do we, George?" Barnard kept staring at Jamie.

"All cut off this morning for repairs, sir."

"So, Mr. Cousins, let me ask you again, in case you've forgotten what we were about to discuss. "What exactly was the true nature of your relationship with the deceased?" Barnard slipped another mint into his mouth, moving it around with his tongue.

"OK. We had a relationship, personal I mean." He smiled. "I'm sure you understand, Inspector. These things happen when you're working closely together."

"Really? Well, I can't say it's ever happened to me, sir." Barnard looked at his sergeant. "You, George?"

"No, sir."

"Well, maybe we don't have Mr. Cousin's gifts with the ladies." Barnard stared at Jamie. "But now we're getting somewhere. A personal relationship, you say. But you didn't think it worth mentioning at our last chat?"

"I panicked."

"Well, you hid it very well, didn't he, George?"

"He did, sir. He seemed to be very comfortable." George flicked open his notebook. "I made a note about it." He turned the pages slowly. "Here it is." He looked up. "Shall I read it out?"

"Yes, George, I think that might help Mr. Cousins here to remember."

"I wrote 'he seems tired, but confident and relaxed'."

"Nicely put, George." Barnard smiled as if a problem had been solved. "That's exactly how I felt at the time." Turning to Jamie, his smile disappeared. "Perhaps, Mr. Cousins, your memory is a little unreliable. So, shall we give it a little test?" He raised his voice, then read through the statement in front of him. "How long had this affair been going on?"

"A few months." Jamie shrugged. "I didn't want my wife to find out."

"Well, I can understand that, can't you, George?"

"I can, sir." Uncrossing his arms, the sergeant leaned forward. "That's understandable. Trying to keep his marriage together. Very creditable."

"Indeed." Barnard started to crunch his mint. "If a little late." He turned his head towards the sergeant. "Do you want to tell him, or shall I?"

"It would come better from you, sir, being the senior officer."

"Quite right, George. Quite right."

"You see, Mr. Cousins, your wife came to see us yesterday afternoon." Barnard stared hard at the man opposite. "She's not very happy with you, is she, George?"

"Not happy at all, sir."

"Why? What did she say?"

"I'm afraid that's confidential." Barnard smiled. "But, as a result of our conversation, we requested your telephone records." He leaned forward. "Obviously, there are a number of calls to

312

the deceased. Understandable, I'd say. Wouldn't you, George?"

"I would, sir. Infidelity is a complicated business. Plans, changes, alibis are needed."

"None after the day before she was murdered." His stare hardened. "Now I think that's a little strange." Leaning further forward, causing Jamie to recoil, Barnard smiled. "You didn't ring her when she failed to turn up for work, nor later in the day. Not even the day after." He stood and slowly walked around to Jamie's side and leaned in as close to him as possible without actually touching. "If I were the suspicious type, I might conclude that you knew there was no point. Because you knew she either would soon be dead or was already."

"No. I…" Barnard held up his hand.

"I haven't asked you a question yet, Mr. Cousins. Returning to his own side of the desk, he picked up the sheet of paper. "What's interesting, though, is there are several calls to an unlisted number." He pushed the sheet in front of Jamie, jabbing his finger at several points. "See? I've highlighted them in red to make it easier for you."

"So?"

"It's a pay-as-you-go phone."

"Probably a customer."

"Of course." Another mint. "A customer. There you are, George. A perfectly reasonable explanation. Why didn't you think of that?"

"We've checked reservations and payment details for customers over the previous two weeks and those booked ahead." George glanced again at his notebook. "It doesn't match any numbers from those people."

"Mmm. Yes. So, Mr. Cousins, we have a problem." Barnard leaned across until he was again just inches from Jamie's face. "And we would rather like your help to clear up the mystery. Especially as one of those calls was exactly fourteen minutes before the young woman was killed."

Jamie's head dropped, but he said nothing.

"That's quite a coincidence, wouldn't you say, George?"

"I would, sir."

"Fortunately, you decided to call again. Yesterday." Barnard took his time extracting another mint from the packet. "Explain it will you, George. All this tech stuff goes right over my head."

"Sir." George leaned forward. "We've been monitoring your calls and have traced the general location of the recipient."

IV

In a first floor, quiet private meeting room provided by the landlord of Doyle's local pub, they sat at the rectangular table, choosing the end furthest from the door. Bottles of both still and sparkling water, with glasses, sat in the middle of the table. Sarah sat next to Louise, whose laptop lay in front of her, with Doyle opposite.

"Right." Collecting his thoughts, seemingly unsure how to begin, Doyle started gently drumming his fingers on the table. "To begin with," looking at both women in turn, Doyle spoke with an accustomed authority in his voice, "I'm sure I don't need to stress the confidentiality angle. All our discussions can go no further until and unless we have the evidence we need." Pausing, he noticed Sarah's gaze darting around the room, while Louise was leaning forward with her laptop open. "Whichever way it goes."

Neither woman spoke, but both nodded.

"So, I have some new information to share." Placing a photograph on the table where both women could see it, he watched for their reaction. "This is a shot from SOCO at the time of their investigations. Fibres can clearly be seen on two branches of a bush." Leaning across, he pointed at the relevant part of the photo. "This was only metres from where Dr Pritchard's body was found. It's a dense area with tightly packed bushes. There were also adult footprints at the same location; I expect to have their full analysis soon."

"They could have been there for some time surely?" Frowning, Louise passed the photograph to Sarah.

"Well, yes. Except the preliminary report suggests that, because of weather conditions, no longer than half-an-hour."

"So, someone else was there." Sarah spoke without looking up.

"Yes, at least they were just before he got there."

"In the middle of the bushes?" Louise frowned. "How many sets of footprints?"

"A number, but all from the same shoes."

"Not a courting couple then."

"You wouldn't get much courting done in there." Doyle smiled. "It's far too dense and prickly."

"Some people enjoy that."

"Then that person would be a witness at least." Speaking softly, Sarah looked directly at Doyle.

"Maybe." Doyle looked at Louise. "You had something?"

"Yes. This is a photograph taken by a student." She passed copies to each of them. "It may confirm what you've just told us." Sarah and Doyle studied the picture. "She took it as part of her college photography course, for a project on solitude. You can see a lone man on the edge of a wood. It's dusk. His face can't be seen, even if we blow it up, because of his hat and scarf, but the background is where Dr Pritchard was found, and this figure is moving away from the woods towards the camera. The date and time are shown at the bottom."

"That's the time of death." Doyle was stunned. "How on earth did you get this?"

"The student brought it to me, after I spoke to her class." Smiling, Louise looked around. "I was a little surprised the police hadn't thought of it. Our college photography course is highly respected and they're always out and about with cameras." Shrugging, she met Doyle's eye. "It was a very long-shot."

"Has anyone else seen this?" Not for the first time, Doyle found himself impressed by Louise's ability to think outside the box. If only some of his officers were as original in their thought processes.

"No. Not to my knowledge."

"Can the image be sharpened up at all?"

"Ahead of you there. Unfortunately, this is the best she could do with it."

"What do we do now?" Sarah's eyes widened, and Doyle heard some enthusiasm in her voice for the first time. "Will this help? It must help, surely?"

"I wonder if there's any CCTV?" Doyle wanted to keep Sarah's hopes under control. Too much optimism could create problems.

"It's possible, although that area is pretty remote." Louise picked up on Doyle's intentions.

"Where was the student standing?"

"By the edge of the field."

"And the figure is heading straight towards her, as far as we can tell."

"Yes." Louise reached over and poured herself some water, Sarah also accepted a glass. Doyle declined with a shake of his head. He was still staring at the print.

"Man or woman?"

"Ana, the student, is definite about that. It was a man."

"Did he walk past her?"

"No. Ana told me he veered off and walked quickly away from her."

Taking a deep breath, Louise made direct eye contact with Doyle. "She got the impression he deliberately avoided her."

"So, we go to that exact place and check out any buildings behind the student."

"There's a road with some houses on the other side, but they're set well back."

"It's just possible someone has a security camera or even a dash-cam. Speak to her again, Louise, get her to take us to the exact spot."

"No problem."

"I have something." Sarah spoke softly, laying a memory stick on the table. "Robert gave it to me the day before he died. I've only just had a brief look at its contents. He told me it's the only one covering everything he found out."

"We can use my laptop."

An hour later, as Louise removed the memory stick, nobody spoke. Stunned, Doyle felt like a bomb had been detonated in the room. Everything he believed changed in that hour. There was now only 'before' and 'after' the memory stick contents. Open-mouthed, Louise said nothing. Sarah began to sob quietly.

"Go through it again." Doyle took a deep breath. He really didn't want to sit through it for a second time but knew he must. "I need to take notes."

"Must we?" Sarah's face was ashen.

"It's impossible. Surely." Staring at the memory stick, Louise ran through what she could remember. But as revelation built on previous information, she had to give up. It was a movie script, a fantasy novel, a doomsday scenario, but surely not a twenty-first century government policy.

After they had been through the contents twice more, all three sat in shocked silence. Words seemed pointless.

"Does anyone know you have this?" Doyle said eventually.

"I don't know." Tears were streaming down Sarah's face. Robert's voice sounded as if he were there with them, that warm tone, the vocabulary, the way he made even the most complex issues sound simple. Struggling to speak as sobs racked her body, she accepted some tissues from Louise. "I'm sorry."

"Take a moment." Louise placed a hand on Sarah's arm. "There's no rush."

"Thank you." Sarah jumped as her phone rang. "It's Emily." Her hands were shaking as she accepted the call. "Hello."

Doyle and Louise watched Sarah's expression, anxious for any clue about the one-sided conversation.

"And you're OK?" A pause. "And they don't mind you staying tonight? Make sure you thank them. Love you too."

Finishing the call, Sarah looked at the other two with eyes full of tears. "Sorry. Emily was just…" Her sobs broke through again. "Sorry… she was letting me know… what was happening."

"No worries." Louise squeezed her arm again. "You should be enormously proud of the way you held it together for her. I couldn't have done it."

"I had to. I can't let Robert down."

"She's safe, yes?" Pulling some more tissues from her briefcase, Louise encouraged Sarah to stand.

"Yes."

"Where's the ladies?" Louise looked at Doyle, indicating Sarah needed some time.

"Left out of here, down the stairs and they're right in front of you."

Waiting for their return, sitting there alone, the magnitude of what he had learned punched Doyle hard in the guts and wouldn't let up. His mind was spinning, repugnance replaced disbelief, outrage made him stand and pace around the room, looking at nothing. A fury like nothing he had ever experienced flooded through him. One part of his brain told him he needed to get a grip before Louise and Sarah returned, another couldn't stop processing the evil that had come to light. He'd never wanted to kill anybody before, but he wanted to rid the world of those who'd created this horror. Sitting down, breathing deeply, he found it impossible to keep still. He stood, stared out of the window, then sat down again. He switched on his phone, then immediately turned it off again. Sitting down for a second time, he looked around the room. Normality was all around, tables, chairs, water. Outside the world would be turning as usual, people moving around normally, in complete ignorance of this atrocity. He felt like shouting at them all, telling them how pointless it was.

Forcing himself to calm down, resisting the temptation to order something strong from the bar, he ignored his notes and waited for Louise and Sarah.

"There's a lot to take in," Doyle said when they came back in, looking through the notes he had been taking. "We need to deal with it point by point." Looking towards Sarah, he wondered how strong she was. "When they searched your house, where was this memory stick?"

"I had it with me."

Making eye contact with Louise, he wondered if her thoughts were the same as his. If they knew about the memory stick, they would still be looking for it.

"If either of you want to drop out now, I wouldn't blame you. As for me, I'm going to do my duty."

"It's an important story and I believe I can help. So, I'm going nowhere."

"He was my husband." Sarah leaned forward defiantly. "I don't know how much help I will be, but I want to stay. For him. And for Robin and Emily."

"OK, then." Doyle looked towards Louise. "We need somewhere to start. Any thoughts?"

V

As Michelle switched on the bedroom light, Jamie's presence startled her.

"So, you went to the police."

"I was trying to help"

"Help who, exactly?" He stood. "Not me, that's for sure."

"I'm sorry. I just thought…"

"You 'just thought'?" He sighed. "I knew you were stupid, but I didn't think even you could be this brainless."

"I didn't give them the book."

"What book?"

Michelle reached inside her handbag and took out Jamie's notebook.

"This. You've made notes of it all."

"Been snooping around in my business, have you?" He made no attempt to grab the book. "You think you're so fucking clever, don't you?"

"I need to get to bed." She tried to move around him.

"Not yet." He pinned her against the wall, his hand around her throat. "It's my own fault. I've allowed you too much freedom, let you do what you wanted."

"Please…" Michelle grasped at his hand. "Please, I can't…"

"Oh, don't you worry." Jamie released his hold. "That'd be too easy."

"You've done something." Breathing heavily, Michelle edged towards the door. "To that poor girl."

"You've read the book." He shrugged. "And if I have, then you should be really afraid now." He grinned, moving between her and the door. "You've caused me much more trouble than she ever did."

"Oh god. You did. You really did."

"You know, Shell. You'd be nothing without me. You'd be on the streets."

"Get out of my way."

"Nope. Ain't going to happen."

Grabbing her hair, Jamie threw her to the floor. She screamed and staggered to the bed. Grabbing the bedside lamp, she used it to hit him hard. He tried to grab it, but she wouldn't let go and just kept hitting until he fell to the floor.

Day Six

Chapter 14

I

Sitting opposite Sir Anthony, Kristina felt more comfortable than on any other occasion she had been summoned to his office. She had followed his instructions to the letter in her meeting with Sarah Pritchard, despite not feeling comfortable with the brief she had been given. Looking around while he dealt with a phone call, she again checked out the wall - mounted photographs, many of which showed him receiving awards. As far as she could tell, there were no additions since she last looked. On the opposite wall, other photos presented him in buddy-buddy poses with recognisable celebrities. Kristina was fascinated by the photograph of Sir Anthony with his arm around Roger Federer's shoulders. His knighthood was conspicuous by its absence from this photographic record, an odd omission she hadn't detected before. The three-seater settee was still by the floor to ceiling window, with its view over the lake in the park opposite. Alongside were a small table and a drinks cabinet.

"What've you got for me?" Finishing his call, Sir Anthony spoke without looking at her, concentrating instead on adding some notes to his iPad.

"She was met outside. I'll text you the car registration."

"Have you traced it?" Looking up, Sir Anthony leaned forward over his desk, his voice icy.

"Of course, I knew…"

"Whose car is it?"

"It's registered to Assistant Chief Constable Doyle."

"That arsehole." Sir Anthony leaned back, veins visibly throbbing in his neck. "Got him." A thin-lipped smile flickered briefly. "Interfering in matters of national security. His career is dead in the water." Pouring some water from the plastic bottle on his desk, Sir Anthony made no attempt to offer any to Kristina. "Get me the private number of the local police commissioner. His chief constable is clearly useless."

"Of course." She had originally intended to ask how the department would be acknowledging Claire's death after her years of unstinting service but decided this was not the time. However, the words she had earlier overheard through his office door had led her into uncovering some troubling information. Kristina had been looking through Claire's office, although it was technically sealed, with even the police prevented from entering. She had found the office keys among Claire's belongings awaiting collection or disposal.

"I've also found out something about Claire's death."

"Leave that alone. It has nothing to do with you."

"I just thought you'd like to know." Wondering why he was obviously so edgy and uncomfortable with the subject of Claire's death,

Kristina was certain she'd made the right decision in not bringing the contacts book and private diary she had found in Claire's office.

"She's dead. That's all I need to know." He moved on. "So, any report from the Pritchard house search?" Sir Anthony finished his water, making no mention of how well she had dealt with Sarah Pritchard. Not that Kristina had expected any.

"No sign of the memory stick, but plenty of other incriminating stuff." Opening her notebook, she wanted this meeting over so she could go through what she had found. "It's all being assessed at the moment."

"Look into getting her for collusion, or assisting a traitor, or any damn thing that gets her locked up."

"Legal services are working on it."

"Right. Then tell them I want her prosecuted, so they'd better find something. Try the unfit mother angle. Whatever it takes."

"I don't think…"

"I don't pay you to fucking think. I pay you to do what I want. Right now, I want that memory stick."

"Of course."

"Phase two is due to start in three days. Nothing must get in the way."

"I understand."

"You understand, do you?" He raised his voice. "Well, understand this. You inveigle yourself into the Pritchard woman's life. You find out where that stick is. And you bring it back here."

"But…"

"No fucking 'buts'. Find it or find another job."

His phone rang. He glared at Kristina. "And concentrate on your job, not on stuff that's nothing to do with you."

Back at her own desk, Kristina reflected on how stressed Sir Anthony had seemed, and worried over his instruction to befriend Sarah Pritchard. This was the polar opposite of his directive about her interview with the scientist's wife and, after that, Kristina couldn't conceive of any possible set of circumstances in which they might share a friendly relationship. Putting that to one side, she flicked through Claire's contacts book and her diary. There was a meeting with someone called Jack, just before she had been hit by the car.

Deciding to get some air, Kristina walked down to the ground floor. Absent-mindedly, she continued to the basement where the building's security was based. About to turn and head back up the stairs, she overheard a conversation that left her shocked. She pretended to be on the phone as a uniformed security guard was talking to his supervisor.

"See, there's the break. All cameras were off."

"Don't worry about it." The supervisor sounded unconcerned.

"But it covers the time of that hit and run."

Kristina pressed 'record' on her phone and moved closer. Both men were looking at a bank of screens and seemed unaware of her presence.

"Listen, Ray." The supervisor, much older than the guard, shrugged his shoulders. "A word to the wise. I like you. You're damn good at your job, but don't start poking around in things that don't concern you."

"But my job is to monitor the cameras."

"Monitor, yes. Invent theories about them, no." The older man pointed to a folder hanging by the side of the screens. "You fill in the log without mentioning this. You make no mention of it at all. Do I make myself clear?"

"Yeah. You do, but…"

"No 'buts, no 'ifs'. Nothing happened, right?"

"Right."

They moved out of earshot and Kristina left the room.

II

Having driven Sarah home, where she collected Emily and a change of clothes, Doyle drove to Louise's house where mother and daughter would stay for a couple of nights. Robin would be away for a further week. Louise and Doyle then collected Ana from her home. Ana was short for Anaisha, she explained, giggling when explaining that in Hindi, it meant 'special'. Her parents had arrived in the UK before she was born; her mother taught biology at the local secondary school, and her father was a chartered accountant with his own business. Photography was one of her main interests and this course was a useful way of spending a year out before studying optometry at Cardiff University.

"So, I was standing here." Ana showed them the viewpoint from where she took the photograph. "And he came from the woods over there."

"He changed direction, you said." Doyle looked around, uncertain about what he hoped to find.

"Yes, he headed off in that direction." Ana pointed to the left.

"That's quite a deviation." Doyle frowned and pointed. "If he intended to go that way, surely he would have taken a different route to begin with."

"Well, a straight line would've brought him nowhere near here," Louise agreed. "Thanks, Ana, can I give you a lift home?"

"No, thanks. I'd prefer to walk." She showed them her camera. "You never know what I might catch."

Once Ana had left, Louise and Doyle followed the direction taken by the stranger. The first exit along that path led towards the town centre through a small area, consisting of a mixture of small local shops, estate agents and two cafes. Residential streets ran off to each side. Several of the commercial premises had CCTV cameras in evidence, and, showing his badge, Doyle viewed whatever footage had been retained.

Nothing stood out, it was just a quiet mid-week evening.

III

Later, over dinner in the pub's restaurant, both Doyle and Louise hid their disappointment and came to a decision.

"We need to approach this from the other end," Doyle said. "This man, Adam Winter. He's the key to this. Pritchard confided in him. That's where we go next."

"Just what I was thinking, chief."

"Still an assistant, I'm afraid."

"Well, what's one initial between friends." Grinning, Louise declined a dessert, in favour of going through the memory stick again. Checking his phone, Doyle had two voicemail messages from the chief constable. 'We need to talk,' was the first. He didn't bother with the second and deleted both.

"There's mention of a woman friend of Adam's and, reading Dr Pritchard's notes, they seem to be very close." Louise turned her laptop around. "You can read the comments – 'Adam talked a lot about Abi, he wants to make sure none of this affects her'. There are more mentions throughout."

"Do we have a full name?"

"We do" Moving around to Doyle's side, Louise paged through the information, impressing him with how familiar she had made herself with these documents. Finding what she wanted, Louise pointed to a line of text. "Here."

"Abi Collier." Reading the name out loud, Doyle waited for Louise to return to her own seat. "Do we know anything about her?"

"Of course, we do. I've been busy." Grinning, Louise talked him through the results of her research. "Dinner's on you, I think."

"It'll be a pleasure." Nodding slowly, Doyle began to relax for the first time since the press conference. "I'll get in touch with the local force. Get them to check out the address."

By ten p.m. they knew Abi had gone away. The local man in charge, Inspector Barnard, was clearly unhappy at being disturbed so late, but also still angry that Abi and her male companion had told him they were going away but had refused to reveal their destination. Describing the details of Sam's murder, along with her relationship with Abi, Barnard stressed they weren't suspects but could still have information vital to the case. Quinn, her companion on 'this little jaunt' was a private investigator. Asked about Adam, Barnard confessed he knew very little about him, other than that he'd disappeared.

"One piece of good news anyway." Scribbling on a page of his notebook, he tore it out and pushed it towards Louise. "We now have this man Quinn's car reg."

"Did you say a PI? Quinn? I'm sure I've heard that name before." Concentrating, Louise re-opened her laptop. "Now where is it?"

"Uh huh." Again, Doyle marvelled at her eagerness to check out every little thing.

Day Six

Chapter 15

I

Hacking sat calmly alongside his solicitor, with Barnard and George opposite. The inspector was already on his third mint.

"So, Let's just go through what we know so far." Clasping his hands on the desk, Barnard stared directly into Hacking's eyes. "We have a witness who claims you paid him for Samantha Watson to be at The Green Man, on the specific day and time that she was murdered."

"Do you have any evidence to support this claim?" Jeremy Page, the solicitor, looked over the top of his glasses.

"Unfortunately, it was paid in cash." Barnard kept his eyes on Hacking.

"Then, my client has no comment to make at present."

"Really?" Loudly crunching his mint, Barnard sighed. "Well, we shall put that to one side for the moment. The same witness also claims to have deposited a large amount of money into your bank account." Pushing a sheet of paper in between Hacking and his solicitor, he watched them both slightly lean forward so they could see the detail. "This amount here." Barnard jabbed his forefinger on the amount being discussed. "Apparently, this was for you to 'make his wife disappear'." He turned to his sergeant. "Those were the words he used, George. Am I right?"

"Spot on, sir. I remember it clearly as it made me think of that magician's trick. The disappearing woman."

"Is this your normal fee, sir?"

"I believed that sum to be an anonymous donation to The Divine Path."

"Now, how did I know you were going to say that?" Sighing, he again turned towards his sergeant. "Did you expect that, George?"

"I did, sir." Flipping open his notebook, he flicked through a few pages before finding the one he wanted. "I wrote it down, sir. Here." The sergeant started to read. "'He will say it was a donation…'"

"That's enough, Inspector." Cutting in, Page shook his head. "My client and I would appreciate it if you stopped playing games."

"Games? I wasn't aware we were playing games." Leaning forward, his face reddening, Barnard stared intensely at Hacking. "This is about the death of a young woman with her whole life in front of her." Barnard's forefinger jabbed the air just millimetres from Hacking's face, causing him to flinch. "A death which you arranged. I don't know why you did it, but I know you did."

"Once again, Inspector, my client has nothing to say in response to your highly emotive accusation."

"George, go through all that tech stuff will you." Leaning back, he slipped another mint into his mouth, before checking how many were left.

"Sir." Once again, George opened his notebook. "You received a call just minutes before Samantha was killed. From our witness."

"You don't need to say anything," Page said before Hacking could speak.

"Tell him about the phone number, George." Barnard stretched out his legs and put both hands in his pockets. "Go on. I will never get tired of hearing it."

"Sir." Again, George checked his notebook. "Well, it was a pay as you go phone, so I suppose you thought it was untraceable. But all modern phones have GPS and this number has been tracked and cross referenced with your normal phone. Both were recorded as being at the same location." Shutting his book, George almost smiled. "Your house. And both were found during our search of your premises."

"You see, Mr Hacking," smiling, Barnard remained relaxed, "the only phones that can't be traced these days are those you buy with cash, use once, wipe, and then throw away."

"I would like to see my client in private."

"Thought you would." Barnard stood. "Come on, George. I expect they have a lot to talk about."

Sitting back in his office and checking his watch, Barnard grinned.

"Fifteen minutes, I reckon. Get the kettle on."

This time, George did smile. But, in fact, it was less than ten minutes.

"Interview resumed at 14.20, Detective Inspector Barnard and Sergeant Baker in attendance."

"My client would like to make a deal, Inspector."

"A deal. Well, now." Setting his mug of tea on the desk, he stretched out and put both hands behind his head. "I can't wait to hear this. Make sure you get every word, George."

"Is this pantomime really necessary Inspector?" Sighing and removing his glasses, Page stared at Barnard. "You have the recording."

"Well, let me ask my sergeant. Is it necessary, George?"

"I think so, sir. Things get lost. Discs disappear. But my notebook remains with me at all times."

"So, I think that answers your question, Mr. Page." Leaning forward, Barnard smiled at the solicitor. "So, what is this deal?"

"My client will provide the name and address of the individual who carried out the attack. And also reveal his current whereabouts."

"Murder," Barnard said. "Let's get this right. It wasn't an 'attack', it was cold blooded murder. It wasn't quick, the young woman suffered prolonged abuse and sustained violence. So, we'll have it right. You'll provide the details of the thug who carried out this vicious murder."

"In return for a lesser charge." Page ignored the inspector's rant.

"I'm not here to make deals." Barnard took a mouthful of tea.

"I'm sure your superior officer will give it serious attention."

"Play golf with him, do you?"

II

Back in his office Doyle was gathering information on the whereabouts of Quinn's car, when the chief constable walked in.

"Ah, Steven." Sitting down and crossing his legs, as always Michael Flint's uniform was pristine. "You've not been easy to get hold of. Did you not receive my messages?"

"Yes, sorry, Mike, I've had a lot on. A few personal issues."

"Well, we mustn't let the personal interfere with the professional." Doyle watched the self-satisfied smile spread across the chief constable's face.

"As you know, sir, I never do."

"Quite so. Quite so." He steepled his fingers with the tips of both forefingers resting on his chin, a habit he had when about to pronounce, usually negatively, on a subordinate's performance. Doyle sat back, knowing what was coming.

"This, erm, this Pritchard case. It seems to have triggered a certain amount of political attention and the commissioner has been on the phone again this morning." He paused. "Is there really anything in it for us? Eh? Just a straightforward suicide from what I gather. Not worth rattling the cages of our political masters, is it? Shut it down, will you. That's an order"

"Sir."

"I trust I've made myself clear?"

"Perfectly, sir."

As the chief constable stood up to leave, Doyle stared daggers at his back. Then he rang Louise. He only needed one final piece of the jigsaw. Traffic cameras had traced Quinn as far as the A171 heading north out of Scarborough. That was enough. Requesting any further information to be sent to his mobile phone, he left the building.

III

Sitting in the park, Kristina waited for Jack Coburn to arrive. After combing through Claire's contacts and her diary, she had decided this was the person she met just before being killed. Having watched them meet on two previous occasions, she knew the location, a fact which seemed to convince the American to agree. Kristina had arrived early, needing time to think through her approach, knowing this was a delicate matter and could easily backfire if she got it wrong.

Exactly on time, Jack Coburn strolled up and sat at the other end of the bench.

"Thank you for coming, Mr. Coburn." Kristina's voice was steady, but her heart was pounding.

"You can call me Jack, and I'm here because you've grabbed my curiosity."

"You used to meet Claire here."

"Did I?"

"Yes. I saw you both twice." Squashing the doubts that were re-surfacing in her mind, Claire breathed deeply. "You met her just before she was killed."

"Did I?" Coburn was staring straight ahead; Kristina noticed he had a coffee.

"I was wondering. I mean while sitting here waiting for you. How did you make sure no one else sat down?"

"Tricks of the trade." Grinning, Coburn turned to face her. "Top secret."

"I need your help."

"You said."

"I admired Claire. She was everything I wanted to be. Strong, resourceful, smart…"

"OK, cut the sermon. Tell me what you want, so I can get on with my day."

"Claire was murdered." She held up her hand as Coburn seemed about to speak. She would only get one chance at this. "I need to say it all. I know the CCTV was turned off. I know it must have been done by someone in our building. Someone senior. I want to find out who and why."

"OK. That still tells me nothing about why you asked me here."

"I thought you might know something. Maybe Claire talked about it."

"Nope."

"Then I'm sorry to have troubled you." Kristina could feel all the fight sliding out of her, all certainty disappearing, and being replaced by a sense of her own ridiculousness. Building up this fantasy until it became believable, real, and important for her to deal with. She wanted him to get up and go, to leave her on this bench, alone with her folly. But he wasn't moving.

"OK." The American accent seemed more pronounced as his voice dropped. "If I can help, I will. For Claire. And yes, you're right on the money. Our own CCTV picked up a black four by four pulling out at that time. Number plates missing." Writing something on the coffee cup side, he handed it to her. "Start here. And you didn't get this from me." Standing and looking around, Coburn fixed her with a stare. "Chuck that away once you've read it. And be lucky." Turning, he sauntered away.

Not moving for several minutes, Kristina stared at the take-away cup, unsure if she had imagined what Coburn had just said. Slowly, she turned the cup around and read what he'd written. 'Cardew' was all it said. Nothing existed for her outside of that name on the cup; she was unable to drag her eyes away from it. Kristina shuddered as icy hands seemed to push and pull at her, and she began to retch. It couldn't be true. But Claire obviously trusted Coburn, met with him regularly. But Sir Anthony? How could that be? He was a bastard, yes, but this? Trying to stand, her knees almost gave way, and she slumped down again.

Eventually she stood gingerly and found movement in her legs. She needed to get back to her office, go through Claire's diary again, try and access her files. Anything.

Sir Anthony's secretary was waiting by her desk.

"Sir Anthony would like to see you in his office." Her emotions summersaulted. Did he know?

How could he? How could she face him? But she had to.

"Fine. Yes. I'll just… One minute." Her voice was shaking; she could hear it but couldn't prevent it. Leaning on her desk for support, her legs almost gave way again.

"Are you alright?"

"Sorry, yes." She clutched the coffee cup to her chest. "Erm, I'll be there in a couple of minutes."

She drank some water from the plastic bottle on her desk, moved papers randomly around and opened drawers without looking into them. Realising she was still clutching the cup, she shoved it into her handbag. Needing to behave normally, she took a deep breath and headed up one floor to Sir Anthony's office.

"Kristina." Greeting her with a wide smile, Sir Anthony indicated she should sit down. If Hacking had been available, Sir Anthony would be following a completely different course, but this would buy him some time. "Now, I've been very impressed with your work in this department."

"Thanks, Sir Anthony." She felt her muscles stiffening; the image of his name on the coffee cup would not go away.

"So, I have some very good news for you."

"Oh?"

"You're being promoted. And you're skipping a grade, with a commensurate increase in your salary. To begin with you'll be on secondment and there will be the usual selection process but that'll be a formality."

"Oh." She tried to get a grip on what he was saying; it had an air of unreality.

"It means moving to a different department and a different building."

"Oh."

"So, forget about Sarah Pritchard and the memory stick. It's no longer your problem." He smiled. "You're moving to food and rural affairs. I've had all your stuff moved into the new office. You'll be sharing, but it comes with a nice pay rise."

"Thank you, Sir Anthony." Dazed and confused, Kristina left Sir Anthony's office

Arriving at her new desk, receiving a curt nod from the older woman with whom she was obviously going to be sharing the office, Kristina began checking through her things. Claire's diary and contacts book were no longer there. She could feel the other woman's eyes watching her. Grabbing her bag, Kristina headed for the nearest underground station, relieved to dump the coffee cup in a bin on the station forecourt.

Standing in the carriage heading home, Kristina's mind seemed to spin with the rhythm of the train. Leaving the station and walking the short distance home, she knew another promotion would delight her parents and a special celebration meal would be planned for the weekend. There was no way she could talk to them about her concerns, they would only worry and ask questions she couldn't answer, so she decided to say nothing other than about the new job. So caught up in these worries was she, that she failed to notice the car that had been following her since she left the station until it drew up alongside her. The rear passenger door opened.

"Get in," said the driver. She recognised the American accent.

IV

Glancing towards Abi as they walked in silence down the hill, Quinn could almost see her mind working overtime. Walking slightly ahead of him, with both dogs on a combined lead, she looked frequently to the left and right, seeing the past, scenes from her time here with Adam. Did they walk hand in hand, Quinn wondered; were they laughing, or worrying about being followed? Maybe they visited one of the small shops, bought ice-cream or a guidebook to the town. He had no way of knowing and Abi showed no interest in talking. They reached the small bay and she leaned on the sea wall, staring through the mist and out to sea. A solitary walker went past, nodding a brief greeting, hiking boots, backpack and stick displaying his credentials for hiking around the east coast cliffs.

After a few moments, Abi turned to Quinn and pointed to the cliffs on the left.

"Adam enjoyed just sitting up there, staring out, looking for ships, pointing out a tanker, a ferry, a yacht." A wide smile spread across her face. "He would say that the Netherlands is over there and Germany that way."

"Good memories." It was all Quinn could think of to say, but Abi didn't acknowledge she'd heard.

"He'll be somewhere in this town." Turning to face away from the sea, narrowing her eyes, Abi gave the impression of looking through every wall, every house, shop, pub, to locate Adam. "I can feel it."

"So, where next?" Starting to feel cold, Quinn wanted the shelter provided by the town's buildings. "Is there a café?"

"Fish and chips." Laughing, Abi started running back up the hill. "Come on. I know where the best chip shop is."

Sitting at a small inside table, next to the steamed-up window, they both tucked in hungrily to their haddock and chips.

"You were right." Finishing his meal, Quinn grinned. "That was great. Best fish and chips I've had for years."

"What next then, Ace?"

"We need a plan."

"Yeah. Duh." Pulling a face that Quinn read as emphasising his stupidity, Abi watched another customer ordering at the counter. Noticeably, she checked out every male figure she saw and, a couple of times, Quinn saw her face light up at a distant figure, only to shut down again as they neared.

"Well, duh." Trying unsuccessfully to repeat Abi's expression, Quinn gave up as she burst out laughing.

"You look like a perv."

"Really? And I suppose you have considerable experience with pervs."

"Yeah. I had this teacher once." Pausing, she grinned and for the first time Quinn noticed her eyes twinkling mischievously. "Looked a bit like you actually. You ever been a teacher?"

"I was once."

"Really, what happened?"

"I got sacked for being a perv." Quinn grinned as Abi's laugh pealed through the room.

"Figures."

"So, any thoughts?" Needing to get their focus back on track, Quinn knew he had to be careful. Green eyes and red hair. Just like Kay.

"Plenty." Letting down her hair and tossing it back, Abi then tied it up again and replaced her hat. "Let's get a drink."

"How is that going to help?"

"OK grandad. It'll help me relax so I can think. It'll be warm. We can't stay here without getting more chips and I'm stuffed." Pushing out her chin, she slid back her chair. "Need any more reasons?"

Sighing, Quinn stood and let Abi lead the way.

Walking back down the hill, Abi pointed out the pub in which she and Adam had stayed.

"Any good?"

"Cosy with great food. And they take dogs."

"Sounds ideal."

Opening the door, they entered a small low-beamed bar decorated with smuggling memorabilia. There were framed copies of documents detailing court cases and the sentences that were handed down.

Various art works around the walls showed clashes between smugglers and revenue men on horses, a horse pulling barrels up the hill, a small sailing boat, looking remarkably the same design as a modern yacht. An old cask stood to the left of the bar, next to an open fire. Barrels were dotted around. Two men, apparently locals, sat cradling their tankards by the fire, a Labrador on the floor between them; they were enjoying a joke with the barman.

"What can I get you?" He came over as soon as they reached the bar, looking pleased to see them. "Bit parky out there." In his forties, Quinn judged. A weather- beaten face and strong hands. Like a smuggler.

Quinn chose a pint of the local beer and Abi had her usual.

"What's the connection with Robin Hood?" Quinn asked, more for something to say, than out of any real interest.

"Ah, now." Placing Quinn's drink on the bar, he leaned across. "If I had a pound for every time

I've been asked that question, I'd be living in the Bahamas."

"You can't even take a bit o' sun, Jackie." One of the locals chuckled. "You'd be back on't plane before you'd left airport."

"You're right there, Bobby." He turned back to Quinn. "Nobody knows. I don't reckon there is one." Turning, he started to pour Abi's drink. "Locals just call it Bay Town."

"I see."

"Down for the day, or staying longer?" Jackie took the ten-pound note proffered by Quinn.

"Not sure yet."

"Well, we've got rooms available." Passing over the change, he started to move away. "Two other couples here already. Just let me know."

"Will do. Thanks." Quinn picked up their drinks.

"Mind yourself on that rug. Sticks up a bit."

"Cheers."

Moving over to a table as near to the fire as possible, without disturbing the other two customers, they sat silently, taking in the place. Watching Abi closely, Quinn again saw her eyes seeing the present but her mind recalling the past.

Not wishing to disturb her thoughts, he glanced through a leaflet advertising various talks about smuggling that took place in the local church hall during the summer months. He idly wondered just how much could be said about a smuggler's way of life, although the list of individual subjects seemed extensive.

"So, Ace. Got a plan yet?"

"Nope. You?" Silently cursing himself for agreeing to this ridiculous exercise in futility, Quinn watched Abi drain her glass. However much she wanted it, whatever persuaded her to believe it could happen, the odds of Adam turning up here seemed as likely as winning the lottery jackpot four weeks in a row with the same numbers. Already, he had seen her hopes crushed as every man in the town turned out not to be Adam. Watching her pitiful expression whenever the pub door opened and Adam didn't appear, was beginning to get to him.

"Another?"

"Of course." Looking up, Abi forced a grin which went nowhere near her eyes.

"Same again?"

"Please." Pulling a ten-pound note from his wallet, he watched the barman, surprising himself with a decision. "And we'll take one of your rooms."

"Grand. I'll just see to this gentleman." He indicated a new arrival Quinn hadn't noticed. "Then I'll come over."

V

After the barman left, Abi stood by the bed.

"Had to be a double, I suppose."

"They had nothing else available, I'm afraid." Shrugging Quinn leaned against the wall next to the door.

"Where are you going to sleep then?" After looking around the room, Abi started to unpack, pyjamas under the pillow, wash bag in the bathroom.

"I'll take the chair, or the bath."

"You're out of luck there, Ace." Closing the bathroom door behind her, Abi grinned. "No bath. Just a shower."

"The chair then."

"You can sleep in the bed." Hands on her hips, legs wide, Abi stared into Quinn's eyes. "Sleep. That's all. Nothing else, understand?"

"Story of my life." Sighing, Quinn checked out the dinner menu.

VI

"Hello, Kristina."

Seeing Claire turn towards her, Kristina felt the shock run through her body.

"What…"

"Sorry for the subterfuge."

"But…I thought…You're not dead."

"I told you she was smart, Claire." Coburn spoke from the driving seat.

"You did. A necessary deception, I'm afraid." Claire smiled. "Jack identified the non-existent body, just in case you're worried I might have bumped off some random old woman."

"We had an American service doctor write up the death certificate," Coburn said in a matter-of-fact voice.

"Yes. I couldn't trust ours." Claire continued to look at Kristina. "All the necessary documents were forged. All the signatures were genuine."

"So," Kristina's mind began to clear. "You must've turned off the CCTV." She spoke softly, almost to herself.

"I did. From my phone."

Kristina stayed silent as she let this sink in.

"And yep, I knew all about it when we met." She saw Coburn's eyes in the mirror. "Sorry."

"What do you want from me?"

"Your help." Claire twisted further around as Coburn parked directly outside Kristina's family home. "Anthony believes he is above the law. That he is the law. Ends justifying means has a real significance when that happens."

"As long as he gets the ends he wants, they're good." Coburn also turned to face Kristina.

"But you were running the first phase." Kristina's mind whirled.

"I was. I thought I could control it." Claire made direct eye-contact. "Make it fail. I couldn't stop it, so that became the only option."

"Did you help that agent run away?"

"No. But I hired Quinn to try and keep it under control. But Anthony was always one step ahead. Hence this performance."

"I don't see what I can do. I've been moved."

"I want you to arrange a meeting with Anthony. Tell him you've got some information about the project and it's worrying you."

"He'll go for that," Coburn said. "If he needs more, then say a newspaper has been in touch."

"Then what?"

"You arrange to meet him in this bar. Don't give him too many options over the day and time. He needs to believe it's urgent." Claire handed over a card. "You'll be sitting inside where he can see you. When he joins you, we'll take over."

"Wait." It was all moving too fast. "Let me think."

"No time." Coburn sounded impatient.

"Give her a minute, Jack."

"So, I just leave when you arrive?"

"Yep. You vamoose."

"Then what?"

"Then you go back to work. Act normal." Claire smiled. "You won't be in any danger."

"Until he comes back."

"He won't be coming back, Kristina." Claire's voice held a hard edge.

"My number." Coburn passed over a card. "Ring when you've got it sorted."

Standing on the pavement, both cards in her hand, Kristina watched the car drive away.

VII

Hacking had spoken to Sir Anthony over an hour ago, as had his solicitor, and he was confident this case would go no further. He just needed to sit tight and delay proceedings as much as possible. At no point did Hacking mention his own interest in adding Christianity to the project; revealing that would certainly prevent Sir Anthony from helping with this immediate problem.

"So, Mr Hacking." Leaning forward, his hands clenched on the desk, Barnard pushed out his most intimidating stare. "It's my opinion that you and whoever you paid to murder this young woman were jointly responsible. Rader is the name you've given us. Do you have an address?"

"Hardly." Hacking smirked. "I don't socialise with these people."

"You have a phone number then?"

"I do. Look, he was just meant to frighten her. I had no knowledge he would go so far."

"And why did you want her frightened?"

"Because of her friend who was becoming a nuisance."

"Her friend?" Barnard turned to George. "Have we heard about this friend before?"

"I don't believe we have, sir."

"Mmm. Strange." Barnard turned back to look at Hacking and his solicitor. "Now, Mr. Hacking, you claim that you had no prior knowledge of Samantha's murder. Is that correct?" Each 'you' was heavily stressed.

"My client has already confirmed that." Grey removed his glasses, twirling them slightly between his forefinger and thumb.

"Yes, well. I'm not as clever as you and I like taking things one at a time. So, if you don't mind, we'll do this my way."

"As you wish, Inspector." Replacing his glasses, Grey jotted down a note on his pad.

"Thank you." He slipped a mint into his mouth. "Now, what you're saying is that you expected her to be, what, roughed up a bit? Maybe put in hospital? Disfigured, perhaps? Something minor like that. Is that correct?"

"Inspector. Once again your language is highly emotive and prejudicial."

"Yes, well." Barnard crunched on the mint. "Murder is a fairly emotive subject, isn't it, George?"

"It is, sir. Hard to observe the social niceties when a young woman has been tortured and murdered."

"So, you see Mr. Grey, we may be a bit bad-mannered and vulgar for your taste, but we have a job to do. And we're going to do it." Turning his gaze back towards Hacking, he lifted his head slightly. "So, perhaps, Mr. Hacking, you would do us the courtesy of answering my question."

"It wasn't that specific."

"Just put the frighteners on, then? Shake her up a bit? Shall we settle for that? Not very Christian, though, is it? What do you think, George?"

"Not Christian at all, I'd say."

"So, you left your Mr. Rader to use his own judgement with this putting the frighteners on?"

"I suppose I did."

"Chief Inspector," Grey interjected, looking over the top of his glasses. "He's not my client's Mr. Rader, and I would appreciate you not naming him in that way."

"Mr. Hacking 'supposes he left Mr Rader to use his own judgement'." Ignoring the solicitor, he turned towards his sergeant. "What should we make of that, George?"

"We could try some supposing of our own, sir."

"Mmm. Yes, indeed we could. Perhaps you could go first, George."

"Sir. I suppose he could be trying to wriggle out of admitting he knew what was going to happen. Or that he planned it."

"Pure speculation, Chief Inspector."

"Well, he started it, Mr. Grey. Anyway, this friend of the deceased, the individual you described as becoming a nuisance," Barnard took his time over choosing another mint, "do you have a name?"

"I do." Hacking glanced towards his solicitor.

"Well, what is it?"

"Abi Collier."

"Abi Collier. Mmm." Looking at George, he saw the same recognition on his face. "So is he likely to have transferred his attention to this woman?"

"I think he may well have done."

"No, that's not good enough. Is he being paid by you to kill Abi Collier?"

"My client has nothing to say at this point."

"OK. Then can you give me a description of Mr. Rader?"

"Skinny, blotchy face, hairy hands."

"Age?"

"Thirty-ish."

"Oh, come on. You can do better than that. Height? Weight?"

"Under six foot. Skinny, like I said."

"I think my client has co-operated to the fullest extent possible."

"Do you? Do you indeed?" Barnard glanced towards George and sighed. "Interview suspended at ten-twenty-two."

Back in his office, Barnard sat for a moment, saying nothing. Then, he looked at George, picked up the phone and rang Doyle to update him.

"He's dangerous. I don't know if he has a weapon. Best to assume he has." Sucking hard on another mint, Barnard ended their conversation with a promise that he would pass on any further information.

"Thanks for the info."

"With Cousins dead, we have no witness." Standing, George bent his knees slightly to try and avoid towering over the chief inspector.

"We have the evidence, though. His statement. That book Michelle gave us."

"Are we charging her, sir?"

"I'll let the superintendent decide that one. Self-defence isn't a crime."

"No, sir."

"I've had enough for one day. Fancy a pint, George? I'm buying."

VIII

Arriving late in Robin Hood's Bay, having followed the tracker, Rader parked his car in a space between Quinn's and the exit. Pocketing his gun and knife, he sneered at the pay machine and strolled towards the sea front. The narrow streets felt claustrophobic, the lack of people unsettling, the absence of traffic unnerving. He wondered how anyone could make money in a place like this; selling ice-cream or tacky smuggling souvenirs would hardly keep him in beer. Where was the action? Some other scam must be going on, he decided, but however lucrative it may be, it wasn't worth living in such a dead shit hole.

Reaching the small bay, he stood alone by the slipway, feeling the cutting wind rushing through him and angry rain pounding into his face. Looking up at the cliffs, he decided that was where he would do it. Up there, with no one around, and an ocean below to get rid of the body. The location was perfect. His instructions were to wait for another man to join Quinn and the girl, then kill all three.

His intentions were slightly different; he was going to kill Quinn and then take his chances.

Remembering why he loathed the sea and felt nothing but contempt for those who flocked to the coast whenever a sunny day arrived, Rader turned up his collar and fought his way towards the nearest pub, deciding he could get nothing done until the following day. Pushing open the door, he swaggered inside in the role of a Londoner, of masculinity, making his way to the bar, where an attractive blonde woman was waiting to take his order.

"A pint of whatever you recommend, darlin'."

"Coming up." Winking, she pulled the hand pump without taking her eyes off him. Strong arms, he noticed, with a red rose tattoo adorning her right forearm.

"From London, are you?"

"Yeah." Handing over a twenty-pound note, he told her to let him know when it ran out.

"Thought so. You have that look about you."

Not having any interest in what she meant, Rader lifted himself on to the bar stool and sipped his beer. It was surprisingly good, much better than he expected.

"Got any more tatts?"

"I certainly have." Turning, she lifted her top to reveal a dragon. "Like them, do you?"

"Yeah. The more the better."

"I've got another one, but I can't show it to you." Grinning, she glanced around the bar. "At least, not here."

"Now you've got me interested." Putting down his pint, he leaned towards her. "Tell me."

"It's a serpent." She also leaned until their faces were almost touching. "Winding its way up my thigh."

"I think I'll book a room."

"Just the one night?"

"Yeah. Don't seem like there's much to do round here."

"You'd be surprised." Pouring another pint, she winked at him.

Having provided a false name, false address, all backed up by false identification, Rader paid cash and accepted a key to room two, the wi-fi code, details of mealtimes and a dinner menu. Other customers started to arrive, so the barmaid became too busy to talk.

Carrying his third pint through to the small restaurant area, he was surprised to see every table was taken. Glancing over the menu, disappointed by the lack of curry, he chose fish and chips. Afterwards, he went back to the bar and ordered another pint.

"On business, are you?" The same woman as before was behind the bar.

"You could say that." Leaning over the bar, he grinned. "A few hours work tomorrow, then back down to the smoke. You ever been?"

"No. I'd love to go. Do the whole tourist thing, you know. Big Ben, Buckingham Palace and I'd love to go on the London Eye." Smiling, she leaned across the bar, picking something off the lapel of his jacket. "I could help you up here. Show you around. Introduce you to some people. Then maybe you'd show me London."

"I don't reckon there's anyone here I want to meet."

"Oh, you'd be surprised." Moving away, she served the drinks ordered by another customer. "What line of business are you in?"

"Security."

"Well, maybe that's just what we need here." Pausing, she took a cash payment from her customer and gave out change.

"I don't reckon there's anything here worth keeping an eye on."

"Well, maybe I can surprise you."

"Unless it's your serpent."

IX

It was Sir Anthony who arranged the meeting.

"So, what can I do for you?" Hacking looked around the room. "This place isn't easy to find."

"I enjoy the solitude and it's discreet."

"It's certainly that."

"I bought this place five years ago." Sir Anthony gazed around. "As a bolt-hole. A place to think and plan. Away from the day to day issues."

"I can see why."

"Guess how much time I've been able to spend here in the last twelve months."

"I've no idea."

"Guess." His voice was sharp, insistent.

"A month?"

"Ha. If only. Two fucking weeks. That's it."

"The cares of state. The kingdom of God does not consist in talk, but in power. 'Corinthians'," Hacking said. "Take time out and allow God to refresh your strength."

"If only. A man like me should be able to get away whenever he wants. But those fucking civil servants can't be trusted. I need to be there, to keep an eye on things."

Hacking said nothing, but didn't, for even a second, take his eyes off Sir Anthony.

"I understand the police are proceeding no further in bringing charges against you?"

"That's correct. You were a great help."

"Then, in my estimation, that makes us even."

Hacking said nothing.

"The way I see it is this." Anthony leaned forward and lowered his voice. "They'll be interested in you for a long time."

"Get to the point, Anthony."

"You've got an escape route?"

"Do I need one?"

"I think you'd be well advised to use one."

"I'm not sure I'm ready for such a drastic measure." Hacking smiled. "I have clients relying on me."

"Listen to me, Hacking. You've fucked up big time. You've no idea what is going to happen now."

"And you do?"

"Oh yes. Shit and fan. And once it starts flying around, who knows where it will stick."

"And you're worried it might all end up on you?"

"I'm not about to take that risk."

"Well, you're the man with the power." Hacking smiled. "Me? I'm just a humble self-employed middleman. A broker offering a service to help solve problems for those in trouble." He paused. "Maybe, I could help you now."

"I don't need your help. Any contact between us now would get tongues wagging in that incestuous Westminster bubble. They love a conspiracy theory."

"You could ride it out. You've done it before."

"You're not going to do it are you?"

"Do what?"

"Disappear."

"Not a chance. And I think you need to calm down. This isn't the time to panic."

"I'm not panicking, I'm dealing with the situation. You should've told me Moss is in your group and that Christianity is being included by him in the vaccines."

"You really have kept your eye on this project." Hacking smiled. "Well, you had to find out sometime, and it does meet your criteria."

"I fucking decide what goes in. Not you. Not anybody else."

"OK." Hacking spoke softly, his eyes fixed on the other man's face. "Would you like to hear my good news? You look like you could do with some."

"Go on."

"I have an operative about to kill your renegade agent."

"That's good news."

"So, we can ride this out. No need for any panic measures."

"Yeah. OK." Sir Anthony stood. "Let's continue this outside. There's a river and the sunset's well worth the effort."

"God's great gift of nature."

"Leave the God stuff out. It's getting on my nerves."

"As you wish."

"So, I have a plan. It doesn't involve you." Sir Anthony spoke as they walked through a small copse. "You really should've considered disappearing for a while."

They stood, looking out over the fast-flowing river. Sir Anthony pointed to the setting sun just sinking below the headland.

"There are worse places to die." With that, Sir Anthony pumped two bullets into Hacking's head and watched as the river carried his body away.

Day Seven

Chapter 15

I

Climbing out of the boat, Adam tucked his papers into the backpack, which he carried rather than wore, and headed into town to find breakfast. His night had been spent tossing and turning restlessly, every little noise bringing him out in a cold sweat. The owners returning was the least of his worries. Abi may have not come, or perhaps she had been and gone; it was at least a week since he left, although he'd lost track of the days. Maybe she'd forgotten their arrangement. Ifs and buts swirled around his mind, making him see stars. Telling himself to focus on things he could control, and not the seemingly infinite possibilities that lay ahead, he went into the first café he found. That was one positive to concentrate on, at least; he still had plenty of cash left.

After the traditional English breakfast with all the trimmings and a pot of Yorkshire tea, Adam felt calmer. It was still early, his watch showed eight-thirty, so he had time to give his papers one final read-through. Abi would still be in bed, and he smiled at the memory of her enjoyment of a long lie-in the last time they were here. Heading for the cliffs, and taking the path just below The Victoria Hotel, he walked up and slowly strolled along the top towards his favourite spot. A fishing boat was heading north, he noticed, and further out, a cargo ship was going in the opposite direction. No one passed him; he hadn't really expected anyone else to be there so early in the morning. Selecting one of the picnic benches overlooking the sea, he set down his backpack and enjoyed the feel of a mild wind wafting around him. Staring out across the North Sea, listening to the waves roaring on to the rocks, Adam watched as a cormorant flew past and drifted down to the shoreline. Birdsong filled in the gaps between the waves, and he began to understand what had always seemed to be a cliché. Nature had healing powers. Feeling lighter, as if he had just shed a great load he had been carrying, Adam felt ready to face his notes and whatever the day had in store. The memory stick was still there, safely stashed in the same envelope Dr Pritchard had given him, a whole lifetime ago. Taking out his notes, secured against the wind by the folder, he began to read them through.

II

Having spoken to Sarah and Emily and making sure they would be fine staying at Louise's for a few more days, Doyle and Louise set off early towards the north east coast.

"I've been looking at this memory stick information again." Opening a notepad, Louise glanced through what she'd written. "I think we've missed an important angle on this."

"Go on."

"If this project is as far advanced as we think, the death of one scientist isn't going to stop it.

The people who want this to happen aren't going to stop wanting it to happen, and they hold most of the aces." Glancing towards Doyle, she looked for his reaction, noticing he stiffened slightly, and his knuckles whitened as he gripped the steering wheel. "And if Quinn and Abi are now going to meet Adam, as we think, then we may not be the only other people there."

"That's a very good point." Deep in thought, Doyle remained silent for several minutes, only speaking again when they reached the motorway. "I could ask the local force to stand by."

"I don't mean to be funny, but if the security services arrive, I'm not sure what a few uniforms will do."

"Point taken." Grinning, despite himself, Doyle lapsed back into silence. "Where's 007 when you need him?"

"He'd be on the other side."

This broke the tension and Louise began to laugh, a musical sensation that ran through her entire body, a sound Doyle had no power to resist and so he joined in. Drying her eyes eventually, Louise forced herself to calm down.

Doyle's mobile beeped.

"Check that will you?"

"Yes, sir." She saluted.

"Habit, sorry."

"Robin Hood's Bay, that's where they are apparently." Looking up, Louise grabbed Doyle's road atlas from the back seat. "I've never heard of it. But the word 'bay' is a giveaway, I reckon it's on the coast."

"Nice work, Sherlock."

They laughed.

III

Having had breakfast, Abi and Quinn strolled down the hill and along the sandy beach to the right of the slipway. There was one solitary individual with a dog walking ahead of them, who every few minutes checked the build-up of clouds. The rain was obviously not far away.

"Buster and Hero would love a run on the beach."

"Go on then, the tide's out."

Looking at each other, they both grinned as the dogs ran full pelt along the sand, chasing each other.

"So, it's almost ten-thirty, how do you want to play today?" Picking up a pebble, he led Abi to the sea's edge, promising her a dazzling display of skimming stones.

"I think lunch-time in the pub is our best chance." Watching Quinn's first throw sink without trace, she began twisting her ring around her finger.

"Not a great stone, that one." Grinning, Quinn selected the pebble that he hoped would redeem his reputation. "Now this is perfect. You know, Abi, my record is twelve skims. South Wales, that was." He paused as memories came flooding back. He hadn't thought about that trip for a long time; it had been his honeymoon. Kay had stood about the same distance from him as Abi did now; she tried to stop her hair from blowing, with the same posture and actions used now by Abi, and both women were grinning and teasing him about his failure to get any stone to skim. Hesitating a moment and looking down at the pebbles, Quinn was unprepared for these memories, having blocked out that portion of his life, yet here it was. On a windy, overcast beach in North East England, rather than a rainy South Wales, his own history was eating away at him. The cottage they had rented, on a farm with an equestrian training centre, the pub where they ate instead of cooking themselves.

Dropping the pebbles and running both hands through his hair, Quinn turned and took Abi's arm before leading her off the beach.

"I never had you down as a quitter." Calling the dogs and attaching their lead, Abi's brow furrowed. "It was only the first go. I bet you'd have done fifteen with the next stone."

"Just leave it."

They continued walking in silence, as the rain started, and they headed for the Bay Hotel bar.

It was just after noon.

IV

When Louise returned from the motorway services with some sandwiches, Doyle waited until her door was closed.

"We have another problem." Taking a deep breath, he stared through the windscreen. "It seems a lone man is also looking for Abi. The chief subject in that murder of Abi's friend. It appears that he's here, and we don't know if he's armed."

"Cheese ploughman's or tuna salad." Holding the wrapped sandwiches for Doyle to see, Louise showed no sign of this new information worrying her.

"Cheese."

"Remind me to never again accept an invitation to help the police." After a pause, she grinned. "Well, in for a penny…"

"You can wait in that hotel over there." He pointed to a Premier Inn. "And I'll meet you when it's done. You still get the story."

"Not a chance." Her smile spread over her whole face. "I want excitement, man. I'm confident in you, I want to see this through. So, let's just get in there like…" She paused. "Like, The Magnificent Two, a budget movie."

Unable to stop himself, Doyle started laughing.

"I didn't think you were old enough to remember that film."

"It was my dad's favourite. Yul Brynner, Robert Vaughn… I can't remember the others."

"Well, we only need two." He said. "Which one are you?"

"You have to be Yul Brynner." Lou pointed to Doyle's thinning hair.

Starting the engine, Doyle steered the car back on to the motorway and accelerated towards Robin Hood's Bay.

V

"Hello, Claire." Sir Anthony ordered a scotch and smiled. "It's a bit early in the day, but hey, it's a reunion. I wondered when you'd show up."

"Really?"

"Of course. You surely didn't think I'd be taken in by your little melodrama?" He stared at Coburn. "I wouldn't recommend Hollywood for a career change after your superiors hear about this pantomime. You just don't have the imagination."

"Thanks for your concern, but I'll take my chances."

"I'm afraid the last chance saloon has just closed for you, Coburn."

"We've traced payments to you from several foreign intelligence services." Claire was determined to get her point across. "You've been selling information."

"Paperwork always was your strongpoint, Claire." He leaned forward. "It's a new world now, there are no secrets anymore, just market forces. Someone wants to buy? There will always be a seller. You and your kind are stuck in the last century. We've moved on."

"I don't believe you."

"I didn't expect you would."

"And you're the man to make it happen?" Coburn said. "Everything has a price. Is that it?"

"You got it, cowboy."

"You sound like a spiv." There was no disguising the contempt in her voice. "Selling bootleg booze."

"Supply and demand." Sir Anthony shrugged.

"Let's cut to the chase here." Coburn leaned forward. "What's your plan now? Here? You haven't come just to boast."

"Oh, good question. You see, Claire, even the cowboy understands."

"Just answer my question." Coburn glanced around. "This place is packed and there are cameras."

"Now, that's good thinking. And I'll tell you." He paused. "By the way, Claire, if you're interested, your renegade agent is in Yorkshire. The east coast to be precise. No need to thank me."

"What do you intend doing with him?"

"Me? Nothing, I've more important things to do. Arrangements have been made to remove him as a problem. Which reminds me." He checked his watch. "Your meddling young disciple will now be in the hands of some very nasty people." He leaned forward. "The project is the only thing that matters. It'll succeed and I'll be here to drive it. You can't stop it. Too many powerful people have invested in it."

"Where's Kristina?"

"Oh, in a basement somewhere. With fewer fingers than she had to start with."

"Leave it, Claire." Coburn put his hand on her arm.

"Do as the cowboy says, Claire." He laid his phone on the table. "In a few minutes two of my men will be here to escort you both to a secure location. I just wanted to say goodbye."

"You really think you'll get away with killing an American citizen?" Coburn said. "One with diplomatic immunity?"

"Now I don't believe I mentioned killing, did I?" Sir Anthony paused. "No, I'm sure I didn't."

"So why are we here?"

"Come now, Claire. Surely you're not that naïve."

"The project." She spoke slowly. "You're going to transform us."

"Bravo." Sir Anthony cheered. "You've surpassed yourself, Claire. I didn't think you'd get it so quickly."

"And your alibi?"

"Oh, I'll be in a meeting with a senior cabinet minister. Not that I'm going to need an alibi."

"What exactly are you intending will happen to us?"

"Wait and see, cowboy." Sir Anthony grinned.

"And what's to stop us just leaving now?"

"Look at the table by the door. Those are my colleagues." He grinned again. "Big blokes, aren't they?"

"They sure don't look like pussycats."

"Nicely put, cowboy. As for you, Claire, you won't be missed. After all, you're already dead."

VI

After leaving Sir Anthony at the bar, Kristina called in sick and went into the nearest coffee shop. She needed to take time out and think. So much had happened. Who could she trust? Who'd believe any of this? Something was nagging at the back of her mind. Sir Anthony had agreed to meeting her much too easily. At the time she was so focused on getting that result, so determined to help Claire, so delighted he'd agreed, that she'd overlooked one thing. He had been expecting it. He wanted it. And not because her explanations were persuasive, or because the potential risk to the project worried him. Kristina was now certain. It had all been too easy, there was no delay in getting put through to him, and he'd agreed before she'd finished speaking. She recognised eagerness in his acceptance of her proposition. That could only mean one thing; Claire was in danger. She had to do something. To at least try. But what? Go back, she decided.

Re-tracing her steps, Kristina peered in through the bar window. The three of them were still there, apparently deep in conversation, Sir Anthony with his back to her.

Inside, she sat down next to him.

"Well, well. You're joining the party, then?"

"Kristina." Claire spoke sharply. "Go. Get out now."

"Too late, I think." He beckoned the two men. "Three of you together. Nice and neat. Much more efficient than dealing with you all separately."

"You need to hear what I've got to say." Kristina stared at Sir Anthony. "I've got everything recorded. All of it. If I don't collect it before six tonight, it'll go to someone who won't be afraid to make it public."

"A superhero to the rescue. You expect me to believe that?"

"Can you take the risk, old boy?" Coburn smiled. "I've seen it. Once it gets out, you'll be up shit creek. And the paddle shop is shut."

"You'd better decide, Anthony," Claire said. "We're getting strange looks from the staff."

"I reckon they're already thinking about calling the cops."

"Where is it?"

"Somewhere safe."

"Don't play fucking games with me." He looked at the two operatives. "You stay here with them. Buy another drink. I'll deal with this piece of shit." Sir Anthony nodded towards the door. "Go on. You're going to take me to it."

"Why should I?"

"That's a stupid question, Kristina. I'm sure you can figure out the answer as we go."

Day Seven

Chapter 16

I

Rader had been distracted by spending the night with the barmaid, Lisa, and had been late getting up. It was midday and he was hungry. Breakfast had finished, but lunch was about to be served. Well, he was in no hurry.

Afterwards, leaving the restaurant and walking outside for a smoke, he saw Quinn and the woman just walking away from the beach with two dogs. He decided to kill the animals first, give Quinn and the woman a sense of what he was about. Grinning, he thought about how much he was going to enjoy this. Going back inside, he went upstairs and packed his bags, transferring the gun into his jacket.

"Hey, stud, you're not running out on me?" Grinning, Lisa pointed to his suitcase.

"Nah. Just getting my stuff into the car. Won't be long."

"I'm all packed and ready."

"Yeah, great." *You ain't going nowhere with me,"* he thought. "Remember what I said last night? About some people I'm expecting. A woman, and one, maybe two, men. Keep an eye out for them."

II

Doyle and Louise had just parked the car when Rader locked his and walked back towards the hotel.

"Skinny, blotchy face." Looking at Louise, Doyle's voice was tense. "Did you get a look at his hands?"

"No. Do you think that's him?"

"I think it could be. Come on." Leaving the car, they followed him down the hill.

It was one p.m.

III

Coburn looked at the two men.

"If we're having another drink, how about some cheese and crackers to go with it? Sort of a last meal."

"Yeah," the taller man said. "Why not? I'm a bit hungry myself."

"I'll order." Stockier than the other man, he went to the bar.

"Get a receipt."

"Ever get called Longshanks?" Coburn gave a friendly smile.

"Don't get clever with me."

"More likely to be Beanstalk," added Claire.

"Your buddy, I reckon you call him Hulk."

"Don't push it."

"Sensitive subject, Jack," Claire said. "Remember your political correctness training."

"Yeah. Sorry, pal. I'm a bit old school."

"Be about ten minutes." Stocky returned with cutlery and a receipt.

Coburn exchanged a glance with Claire.

"You ever watch Toy Story?" he said.

"Yes," Claire replied. "There were four, I seem to remember."

"Yeah. Three was good."

"I preferred two."

"The best though, was one."

On the word 'one' both Claire and Coburn grabbed knives and stuck them through one hand of each of the men. Kicking the table away, Coburn punched Stocky in the face. Lofty was struggling to free his hand from the table.

"Sorry, lads." Coburn grabbed Claire's arm and they ran from the bar. "Glad you picked up on Toy Story."

"I'm surprised they didn't," Claire replied. "Don't they teach them anything these days? The countdown trick was one of the first things we learnt."

"Where do you think she'll take him?"

"The office, maybe."

"Would you go back there with a building full of people keen to suck up to their boss?"

"Good point." Claire stood still. "Wait. Let me think. I'd go somewhere I felt safe, where no one else would get hurt."

"OK. So where?"

"Her local church." She spoke almost under her breath. "That's it. She plays the organ at her local church. That's where she'll be going."

"OK. You're sure?"

"I have to be. We'll only get one shot at this."

"My car's over there."

Day Seven

Chapter 17

I

Adam walked slowly towards the Bay Hotel bar. Having made it this far, got this close, he felt the panic rising. Thoughts swirled around his head, he began to have palpitations, and he was sweating. Uncertainty clawed at him for the first time since he ran. Abi would be here, he felt it. But how could he face her? How could he tell her of the things he'd done? She wouldn't see him in the same light as before. How could she? What would he do if she rejected him? He stood motionless and tried to think calmly. She'd understand. But why hadn't he told her before? All those lies. Abi hated liars. Then he couldn't see properly, all those missions burst into his mind, mingling and morphing into a furious Abi. Adam couldn't go through with it. Not now. He needed time to think.

Returning to the much busier café, he ordered coffee. It was one p.m.

II

Abi and Quinn sat in the bar, Abi listening to Quinn's explanation for being so abrupt earlier.

"I didn't realise you'd been married."

"You find it difficult to believe?"

"No. Not that." She sipped her drink and grinned. "Although, it's hard to imagine a real woman falling for you."

"Yeah. Yeah. I know."

"It was a real woman, right?" She grinned.

"Very real." Shuffling uncomfortably, he picked up the menu. "That sea air has given me an appetite. Shall we eat?"

"Of course."

It was one-thirty p.m.

III

Rader checked each pub or café that he passed, The Bay Hotel being the closest to the sea and his last possibility. This was good, he decided. So close to the cliffs. Easy to get them up there. Peering through the window, he saw Quinn and the woman sitting at the far end of the bar. He grinned. There were three other customers he could see, two sitting at separate tables and one at the bar. Not ideal, he decided. He'd give it a few minutes.

It was one fifty-five.

IV

"He's obviously looking for someone." Doyle spoke as they watched Rader check buildings as he passed. "That's him alright."

"What's the plan, chief?"

"We wait until he's off-guard," he said. "He'll be keyed up at the moment. On his guard. If we approach him now, we'll be spotted straight away."

"He seems to have stopped looking." Lou nodded in the direction of The Bay Hotel. "I reckon he's found what he's looking for."

"Then the two targets must be in there." He looked around. "We can get a bit closer. Cross over and walk towards that information board by the sea wall."

"I should call for back up."

"I don't want to rain on your parade, chief. But, if he'll be spooked by us, a dozen armed officers isn't going to calm him down."

"I know." Doyle grinned. "Just thinking out loud."

The church clock chimed for the hour.

Two p.m.

V

With Coburn's high-speed chase training, they reached the church Kristina attended within minutes. The front door was locked.

"We'll never get through that without explosives."

"There's always another way into these places." Claire checked around. "Got it. Jack, over here."

"Now that's more like it," he said. Within seconds he'd broken the lock and they were inside. Steps took them down into a crypt full of religious iconography, coffins, and memorial stones

"What's that smell?" Claire whispered.

"I don't reckon we want to know."

At the far end was another door, which wasn't locked. It opened easily and they stood still, listening to two voices.

"Over there." Coburn pointed.

Kristina and Sir Anthony had their backs to them. He was facing her and looking through some documents, she had been tied to a pew.

"Well, you've been very thorough." He slapped her hard across the face.

Claire stiffened.

"Is this the only copy, bitch?" Anthony's face was inches from Kristina.

Coburn had the gun in his hand.

"Legs," said Claire.

Two shots echoed, Kristina screamed, and Sir Anthony fell to the floor. Before he had chance to react, Coburn had him in handcuffs.

"Come on, Kristina." Claire spoke gently, an arm around the younger woman's shoulders. "It's over. You're safe."

Kristina burst into tears.

VI

Rader watched as two customers left the bar. That was good enough. He burst in, with as much noise as possible.

"You two," he waved his gun at the barman and the other customer, "on the fucking floor. Hands behind your heads. Or I'll blow your fucking faces away."

Quinn started to move.

"Stay where you are, hotshot. Remember me?"

"Yeah."

"We're going for a little walk. Get a bit of fresh air. Bring the slag." He waved his gun towards the exit.

Outside, partly hidden on the slipway, Doyle and Lou watched Rader leading Abi and Quinn at gunpoint along the cliff path. Buster and Hero were on leads.

"We follow," Doyle said.

Then time seemed to stand still. A scream cut through the air.

"No. No. No."

Adam tore up the space between himself and Abi, zig zagging as he ran, flinging his backpack to one side.

Rader fired but missed. He pushed Quinn and Abi to the ground and fired again three times and Adam fell to the ground, just two metres from Abi. She had almost touched him.

Quinn rugby tacked Rader and the gun flew out of his hand as he hit the ground. Doyle and Lou arrived.

"Now call for back up, Lou."

Abi knelt by Adam's body. Buster went to sit by her, then Hero arrived alongside his friend. All three sat in silence.

Day Twenty

Chapter 18

I

"I think I'll stick around for a bit, if that's OK?" Quinn said as he and Abi walked Buster and Hero.

"What for? I don't need looking after."

"Just 'til after the funeral."

"Whatever." She stopped walking and turned to face Quinn. "He saved my life, but now I find out he wasn't who I thought he was."

"He saved your life. What more do you need?"

"What'll happen to his killer?"

"Prison. For a long time."

They walked on.

"I picked up his backpack."

"I saw."

"You know what's in there, don't you?"

"I have a pretty good idea."

"Will you go through it with me?" Abi asked. "I want to finish whatever he started." She paused for a moment. "He was a good man. Whatever he did, I'll never believe he was anything else." She held up her hand as Quinn began to speak. "No. Wait. I knew him. The real him. I can't let his life be for nothing."

"Can I say something?"

"It depends what it is, Ace."

"If you're sure you really want to do this, then I'd like to help. And yes, he was a good man trying to put right a mistake."

"We'll start with the backpack, then. There's a thick hand-written document and a memory stick."

II

"Hello, Mrs. Pritchard. Thanks for seeing me. How are Robin and Emily?"

"Fine, thank you, Kristina. They're so much more resilient than me. Robin's following in his father's footsteps. Emily's not sure what she wants to do yet."

"Well, I'm really pleased they're doing well."

"Thank you. And please call me Sarah." They sat facing each other. "I've heard such remarkable things about you."

"Oh…, erm…, yes…, thank you." Kristina blushed. "I don't really want to talk about it, if that's OK?"

"Of course."

"I just wanted to say I'm sorry about when we last met… the interview, I mean…I feel bad about the way I spoke to you. It was horrible."

"Well, it was a bit of a shock." Sarah frowned. "Please don't say you were just following orders."

"I have no excuses."

"You were placed in an invidious position."

"I handled it badly." Kristina made eye contact and held it. "I should've been stronger."

"It seems to me," said Sarah, "that you've more than made up for any weakness at that moment." She smiled. "So, I want to forget about it. Move on. Keep Richard's name alive."

"I'd love to help."

"I was hoping you'd say that." Neither woman spoke for a few moments. "And what about you? Are you fully recovered from your ordeal?"

"I think so."

"I'm very pleased to hear it." Sarah stood. "Just stay there a minute, Kristina."

"Yes, of course."

Returning after a matter of seconds, Sarah handed the memory stick to Kristina.

"We have work to do. This is what Richard would've wanted."

III

"There was a point when I didn't think we'd ever get here." Claire sipped her wine as they waited for the main course to arrive.

"Only one?" Coburn said. "Jeez, you're one tough cookie."

"Well, we made it."

"Yeah." He leaned forward and lowered his voice. "What's happening to Cardew? I've heard nothing and if I start asking questions the shit really will hit the fan."

"He's taking some leave, but with friends in high places, he'll be back."

"No charges at all?"

"Those in power need him, because they still want the project to go ahead."

"For real?"

"I'm afraid so. He's become indispensable. And they're all scared of him."

"This is legit, right?"

"I'm afraid so."

"Do you know where he is?" Coburn leaned back as the food arrived.

"It's classified." Claire smiled. "They won't trust me with anything like that."

They lapsed into silence and started to eat.

"We can't just back out now, Claire."

"I was rather hoping you'd say that, Jack."

IV

"Lou." Doyle stood as she entered the coffee shop. It seemed a lifetime ago that they had first met here. "I was intrigued by your message. A proposition, you said."

"Yes. We have some unfinished business."

"Ah, yes. I had a feeling you wouldn't leave the Robin Hood's Bay events behind."

"I can't. Can you?"

"Haven't you heard? I've retired."

"I heard."

"Yet here you are."

"Here I am."

"Tell me what you have in mind," Doyle said. "I must admit to being slightly bored already with retirement."

"You heard I've moved into national radio news?"

"I did. Congratulations. It's well deserved."

"Thank you," Louise paused. "Well, I've got a bit more freedom now."

"And you want to follow up on that memory stick?"

"See." She grinned. "You maybe retired, but you've still got it."

"Some things you can never get rid of."

"You see, Chief." Lou leaned forward. "We both saw the horrific information on that memory stick. We can't just stand by and let it happen. It's nothing less than genocide. The man who was killed, in front of us, he was one of their first experiments."

"He was."

"I can't leave it there."

"You're looking for more personal glory, are you? All in the cause of your career, is that it? TV next, I suppose?"

"You bastard. That's unfair."

"It's what it looks like to me. A scoop, an exclusive, TV reporter of the year."

"I'm sorry. I've made a mistake." She stood. "You're not the man I thought you were."

"Sit down."

"Why should I?" She glared at him. "This won't work. I thought you were better than this."

"Stop sulking and sit down."

"Don't patronise me. I've had enough of white men treating me like shit."

"OK. OK. Relax. I get it. This has nothing to do with your skin colour, or the fact you're a woman. Please, just sit down," Doyle said. "I want to be sure you know exactly what you're getting into and the risks involved. I couldn't forgive myself if you got hurt."

"I don't need your protection. I'm perfectly capable of looking after myself."

"Yes. Of course," he replied. "Forgive me. Sometimes old habits die hard. I know very well you bring more to this investigation than I do."

"Nothing to forgive. I'm a bit sensitive, sorry. Shall we start again?"

"Please."

"So, we need to get in touch with Sarah Pritchard. She should still have the memory stick."

Printed in Great Britain
by Amazon